A SOUTH BEA

According to our source[...] in the services industry, the long-standing accountant at celebrity hotspot Brittany Beach has skipped town. No word yet on how much of Brittany Garrison's money the money counter may have taken with him on what is sure to be a long vacation. A spy at a popular beachside restaurant reports that the youngest Garrison sibling is searching for a financial backer to bail her out of her latest disaster and that she won't turn to her wealthy siblings for help.

And that might be for the best. Another source informs us that the Garrison clan is still reeling from the discovery of a sixth sibling—an alleged product of one of Old Man Garrison's affairs. A close family confidante reports that the

[...] owns a chunk of Garrison, Inc. and is willing to play hardball with reformed-for-now playboy Parker Garrison in order to keep her shares.

In other SoBe News, we hear the Jefferies Brothers are looking to expand their business ventures once again. Seems the recently opened boutique lodging of Hotel Victoria wasn't enough competition for the once-popular, now-not Garrison Grand. No word yet on where the breathtaking bachelors have set their sights this time.

Dear Reader,

In spite of ambition, deception and family loyalties, the power of true love can triumph over everything else. This is a story of such a love that grows between a man and a woman. On an August night in Miami, when Emilio Jefferies walks into Brittany Garrison's life, he changes it forever, as well as his own. A partnership binds the two together. Brittany, one of the youngest Garrisons, falls in love with the handsome playboy whose destiny becomes linked with hers and passion burns hotly between them.

Obstacles to Brittany and Emilio's happiness abound as an agreement is forged based on lies, driven by ruthless ambition and almost destroyed by family feuds. Even the powerful Garrison dynasty becomes a barrier to them. In spite of this, the love, respect and friendship that builds between Emilio and Brittany is strong enough to triumph over the pitfalls and the disasters that threaten to destroy them. This story is a reaffirmation of love's strength to conquer all.

Please enjoy,

Sara Orwig

SARA ORWIG

SEDUCED BY THE WEALTHY PLAYBOY

Silhouette® Desire

Published by Silhouette Books

America's Publisher of Contemporary Romance

A very special thanks to Jana Amsler,
owner of Salbute, in Hinsdale, Illinois.
Also, many thanks to Melissa Jeglinski, Demetria Lucas,
Roxanne St. Clair, Anna DePalo, Brenda Jackson, Emilie Rose,
Catherine Mann—you've been great to work with!

Special thanks and acknowledgment are given to Sara Orwig
for her contribution to THE GARRISONS continuity.

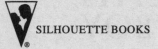 SILHOUETTE BOOKS

ISBN-13: 978-0-373-76813-4
ISBN-10:   0-373-76813-3

SEDUCED BY THE WEALTHY PLAYBOY

Visit Silhouette Books at www.eHarlequin.com

Printed in U.S.A.

Recent books by Sara Orwig

Silhouette Desire

Do You Take This Enemy? #1476
The Rancher, the Baby & the Nanny #1486
Entangled with a Texan #1547
†Shut Up and Kiss Me #1581
†Standing Outside the Fire #1594
Estate Affair #1657
‡Pregnant with the First Heir #1752
‡Revenge of the Second Son #1757
‡Scandals from the Third Bride #1762
Seduced by the Wealthy Playboy #1813

Silhouette Romantic Suspense

*One Tough Cowboy #1192
†Bring on the Night #1298
†Don't Close Your Eyes #1316

*Stallion Pass
†Stallion Pass: Texas Knights
‡The Wealthy Ransomes

SARA ORWIG

lives in Oklahoma. She has a patient husband, who will take her on research trips anywhere from big cities to old forts. She is an avid collector of Western history books. Sara has a master's degree in English, and has written historical romance, mainstream fiction and contemporary romance. Books are beloved treasures that take Sara to magical worlds, and she loves both reading and writing them.

THE GARRISONS

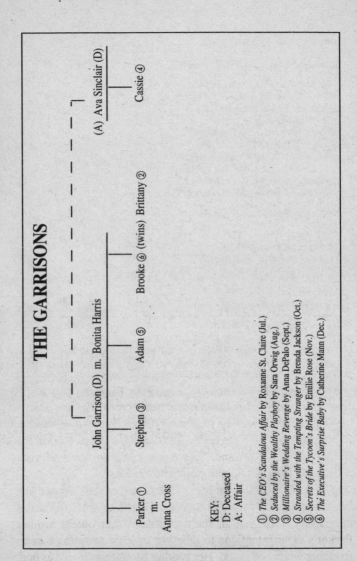

John Garrison (D) m. Bonita Harris

- - - - - - - - - (A) Ava Sinclair (D)

Parker ①   Stephen ③   Adam ⑤   Brooke ⑥ (twins) Brittany ②   Cassie ④
m.
Anna Cross

KEY:
D: Deceased
A: Affair

① *The CEO's Scandalous Affair* by Roxanne St. Claire (Jul.)
② *Seduced by the Wealthy Playboy* by Sara Orwig (Aug.)
③ *Millionaire's Wedding Revenge* by Anna DePalo (Sept.)
④ *Stranded with the Tempting Stranger* by Brenda Jackson (Oct.)
⑤ *Secrets of the Tycoon's Bride* by Emilie Rose (Nov.)
⑥ *The Executive's Surprise Baby* by Catherine Mann (Dec.)

One

Brittany Garrison's life had catapulted into disaster. As she stared at the books spread in front of her, she broke out in perspiration even though she was chilled to the bone.

"Now I know why my accountant disappeared," she whispered. If only she had known about Paine Elsdon's embezzlement of two million dollars before his mysterious disappearance, it might have been possible to catch him.

"There's no escaping the truth," Boyd Dumont remarked. "The money could have been deposited into an account in the Bahamas or Switzerland. Your former accountant and your money are long gone from South Beach Miami."

She barely heard what her new accountant said. Seated at a table in his quiet office, Brittany couldn't stop thinking about her family. Last month, she'd overheard her oldest brother Parker's clear intentions to take her upscale restaurant away from her when she failed. Her brother Stephen was just as bad.

Stephen's remarks that she wasn't competent in business drummed in her ears with each heartbeat. Brittany Beach was a growing success. The numbers were there in black-and-white.

"Paine must have been embezzling funds from the start," she said, unaware she spoke aloud. "I trusted him because he came with excellent references."

"This could be the first time," Boyd speculated. "Maybe he got into a pinch and took a little, just to borrow it. Once he crossed that line, he kept on." Boyd shrugged his narrow shoulders as the light glinted on his glasses. "I suspect you won't find him."

"How did he get away with this?" she asked, stunned by the deception of someone she trusted. "The books looked fine."

"Your accountant doctored the books. My guess is, he may have had two sets of books. One for you and another one that he kept."

Her fingers drifted lightly over the cleft in her chin that marked every Garrison sibling. "Let me figure out what to do before there's any publicity," she said, thinking it wasn't public awareness she wanted to avoid, but the knowledge of her family. "We'll notify the law, of course."

"Certainly. But you can't wait long before you have to make payroll, buy supplies and meet the endless expenses of a restaurant."

As if she could wipe away her pounding headache, Brittany rubbed her temples. She should be worrying about how to manage so much debt. Instead, all she could think of was family humiliation. They viewed her, the baby of the family, as incompetent. Even Brooke, her twin sister, regarded her as inept. Now, if she didn't do something quickly, she was going to prove them right.

"Temporarily, other than the authorities, I don't want this embezzlement to go beyond this room."

Boyd nodded his bald head. "My work with all my clients is confidential. But I believe you told me that some of your staff discussed your accountant's mysterious disappearance. Even if you don't hear them, there will be rumors and speculation."

Realizing Boyd was right, she drew a deep breath. "Word travels in the restaurant industry like wildfire," she remarked, pondering her dilemma. "There has to be something I can do," she said, wondering how she could get the capital necessary to keep afloat.

"Brittany, if I may say so, your brothers can bail you out. Even with this immense debt you're in, they're quite well fixed."

"That's what I'm worrying about," she admitted, biting her lower lip. "I want to solve this problem myself."

Boyd sat in a vinyl chair at the head of the table. "That's a noble ambition, but you're going to have to be practical. They'll wonder why you didn't come to them. And it would cost you the least."

"No," she said emphatically, shaking her head. If Parker learned about the embezzlement, Brittany Beach would be gone as if taken by hurricane winds. Parker was a control freak who oversaw all the Garrison holdings. He already wanted her restaurant because the family retained the land, which was one of the last prime pieces of oceanfront property zoned for condos. She knew Parker envisioned condos that would bring in more money than her restaurant.

She rubbed her chin. "Go through this again with me. It's impossible to accept." An hour later, she left his office in a daze.

A week later, Brittany stood in the art deco dining room of Brittany Beach while she talked to her director of services, Hector Garland. The disaster that had come into her life nagged her and she couldn't keep her mind on Hector's conversation. Lost in her own thoughts, she looked around.

From the appearance of the restaurant, no one would guess there was the slightest problem. The cobalt ceiling with soft lights was a contrast to dusky pink walls. Candlelight flickered and bouquets of flowers graced the room. Eating areas, where patrons could lounge while they ate, were cushioned in Haitian white cotton. Cocktail waitresses moved around in colorful halter tops and low-slung sarongs. Outside the main dining room was a partially covered veranda, and beyond the white-washed planks were white cabana tents on the beach. Each tent contained sofas for lounging and eating.

How could such an inviting place be a quicksand of catastrophe for her? Brittany couldn't stop wondering about what she was going to do to save the restaurant and herself.

As she tried to concentrate on what Hector was saying, she noticed a tall, dark-haired man standing in the lobby. She recognized Emilio Jefferies and knew he operated El Diablo, a small, exclusive and popular Cuban restaurant in SoBe that also catered to Miami's jet-set crowd. She had seen her competitor's name and his picture in tabloids, seen him at local happenings and they had met briefly at restaurant events. While she watched, her maître d', Luis Munoz, spoke to Emilio Jefferies and turned to lead him to a table.

When Emilio crossed the main dining room, he moved with the ease of a panther, Brittany thought, watching his long legs and his easy, relaxed stride. In a navy suit and white shirt, he stood out in spite of a clientele of jet-setters, models and buff studs. She knew from Emilio's press coverage that he was thirty-three and definitely single.

"What's he doing here?" Brittany asked her services director, who turned to follow her gaze.

"I suppose he's curious about us," the slender black-haired man replied. "He's eaten here before. Every month we're having more business. Let's hope we grow to rival El Diablo."

She tried to smile, but found it impossible. More business. Less money. She rubbed her hands together, yet she couldn't stop watching Emilio.

"Excuse me, Brittany," Hector said and hurried away.

Barely hearing Hector, Brittany didn't take her gaze from Emilio. He was more handsome in person than in his pictures.

Luis seated him on one of the curved chairs that faced a spectacular view of the white beach. Luis talked to him briefly and left. When Emilio was alone, his gaze circled the room. He looked into Brittany's eyes.

Her breath caught and she stared at him while he nodded and smiled in acknowledgment. She was held by his commanding gaze. With an effort, she smiled in return and then strolled to a table to chat briefly with patrons. Her back tingled and she wondered if Emilio's eyes followed her.

In a few minutes, she left the dining room to return to her corner office, stepping into the spacious room with its polished hardwood floor, teak desk and rattan furniture cushioned in the same Haitian white cotton as the restaurant's other furnishings. A glass wall provided a spectacular view of the private part of the veranda and the beach beyond it. At one end of her office was a long teak-and-chrome table where she worked.

When she was seated at her desk, she pulled up her list of possibilities for funds and read it over again, knowing there was nothing promising. If she didn't do something in the next week, the restaurant was going under.

After racking her brain and coming up with no solution, she went to her private bathroom and looked at herself in the full-length mirror. The brightness of her fiery-red skirt and red silk blouse mocked her dying future as owner of Brittany Beach. Her long brown hair was caught in a clip with tendrils hanging loose and curling around her face. The image in the mirror didn't look like a person facing disaster. She smiled at herself, while inwardly, she churned with worry.

Satisfied with her appearance, she squared her shoulders to return to the main area. When she entered the room, her eyes immediately went to Emilio, who still dined alone. She chose to greet her other guests instead of heading straight to his table as she wanted to do.

It was another fifteen minutes before she approached him. He came to his feet and that riveting moment when she had locked gazes with him across the room was nothing compared to looking directly into his thickly-lashed, crystal-green eyes. She couldn't resist a swift glance over him and was immediately aware of his height. She was tall, herself, nine inches over five feet, yet he was at least six inches taller. His olive complexion added to his rugged appeal, yet it was the aura of sensuality that took her breath more than his physical appearance.

"Please, sit," she said.

"If you'll join me," he replied in a gravelly deep voice that heightened his magnetism. "I've finished eating. Have a drink with me."

"Thanks," she replied. As she started to sit, he came around to hold her chair. When they faced each other, she smiled at him. "Welcome to Brittany Beach. You checking us out to see what the competition is doing?"

"Sure, but I also enjoyed a fine dinner," he replied. She glanced down to see he'd had crab legs with melted butter.

"One of my favorite selections. I hope you've enjoyed your crab."

"I did, but my evening just got better."

She smiled. "I'm sure you flirt as easily as you breathe," she countered, noting an electrifying tension snapping between them. Now she could understand how he so easily attracted women.

"How can I resist?" he rejoined, his deep voice lowering slightly.

"You've been here before."

"Yes. The food is always good, so I come back occasionally. My compliments to your chef," Emilio said, smiling at her with a flash of even white teeth. Creases bracketed his mouth and his handsome appeal increased exponentially.

"Thank you and I'll tell him. Do you always check out your competition?"

"Sure. I'd guess you do, too, and I'd be willing to bet that you've eaten at El Diablo."

"As a matter of fact, I have. The food was also excellent."

"Thanks. I see we draw the same crowd, so we're direct competitors, but you're my most beautiful competitor, no question."

With a jump in her pulse, she smiled at him, yet she suspected he would put Brittany Beach out of business without a qualm if he could. "Thanks, again. I think there's room in SoBe for both of us," she replied tactfully.

"At least until you take my clientele," he answered lightly, smiling in return.

She laughed. "Our restaurants are sufficiently different. You carry dining to a more sensual level than we do here," she replied.

He glanced around and shrugged. "Everything in here is sensual—the ambience, the ability to lounge while you eat, great food, the very attractive waitstaff, music that has a primitive beat. No, I don't think I have the corner on what's sensuous, Brittany."

He said her name in his husky voice that stirred a tingle in her. She enjoyed sparring with him, feeling sparks dance between them, yet she suspected that her reaction was the same as every other female he encountered. The man reeked sex appeal and she was intrigued that he found her enough competition that he would make himself known at Brittany Beach. Or did he have some other reason for his presence?

"I should get you to write our ads," she answered, wondering what was really on his mind. Or was she reading too much into his visit?

"I could do your ads," he said with another flash of his white teeth. "Brittany Beach, fine dining taken to a new level of sensuality by its gorgeous owner."

Smiling, for a fleeting moment she forgot her worries about her finances. "You exaggerate, but I think I'm going to enjoy having you for a Brittany Beach patron," she replied with a toss of her head.

"Next time, join me for dinner," he suggested and she nodded.

"Whenever you want," she answered. "Unless there's a kitchen crisis or some reason I'm needed elsewhere. I see you're through eating. Would you like your own tour? Or have you already seen everything there is to see?"

"Not even remotely," he answered with a twinkle in his eyes. "I suspect there's a lot more to learn about." His tone suggested something more personal than the restaurant. "Let's do it," he said. "I'm already fascinated. I can't wait to see what else you'll show me."

She was amused by him, flattered, even though she was certain every woman he was around received the same flirting and compliments and she knew she shouldn't put stock in anything he said. She suspected he would look around, flirt some more and leave and she wouldn't see him again unless it was at restaurant functions or SoBe events.

He came around to hold her chair and fell into step beside her as she began the tour. She was aware of him close at her side.

"You know we're in the main dining room and you can see the cabana tents beyond the veranda. Off the dining room in this direction are the private rooms and, tonight, all but one are already filled," she said, motioning toward an open door and leading the way inside a small dining area with four long tables. "We can rearrange the tables to accommodate fewer or more than this. Now over this way," she said, leaving the room and switching off the light behind her, "is the lounge. We'll have strobe lights, hip-hop on some nights and, nearly always, hot bodies."

Even as she talked, the music grew louder and they stepped inside the darkened area briefly to watch dancers while the fast music drowned out possibilities for conversation. She touched his arm lightly because she had to raise her voice to be heard over the music. His head swung around and she motioned back toward the hall.

She took him on the rounds of public areas, avoiding any of the private parts of the restaurant and when she had finished, she turned to face him. "There, you've seen Brittany Beach. Would you like to go back to your table or maybe outside? It's cooled somewhat by this time of night."

"Only if you'll join me," he replied, and she shook her head reluctantly because she had enjoyed being with him, but she had already taken a lot of time away from work.

"I'm on duty, actually, and I might join you later, but for the time being, I need to keep checking that everything is running smoothly. Thursdays are busy."

"In that case, I'll call it a night. But I want to talk to you privately. How about an appointment tomorrow?"

Surprised, she wondered what was on his mind that he couldn't have already asked her or talked to her about. She shrugged.

"Sure," she said. "We can set an appointment, or I can take a little longer now and we can go to my office," she replied, curious.

"Right now is fine if you have the time," he replied easily.

"My office is back this way," she said, directing him to a

hallway. Once again, she noticed his height as he walked beside her. They exited the crowded dining room to stroll into a hall where thick blue carpet silenced their steps. In the glass-enclosed reception area for her office, a small light burned.

Crossing the room, she opened the door. When she switched on a dim light, he moved to the middle of the room and pushed open his coat to place his hands on his narrow hips as he looked around. "Nice office," he said. He ran his hand along the edge of her free-form teak desk and she watched his well-shaped fingers slowly, sensuously, rub the smooth surface. "Cool desk," he said.

"Have a seat. Would you like a drink?"

"No thanks," he answered, circling the room to look it over. He dominated the space and she knew the image of him in her office would stay with her.

"We share the same taste in art," he remarked, looking at a Mondrian. "Excellent choices in paintings."

"Yes, I prefer modern art, too. I've seen you at galleries. Take off your coat if you'd like," she said.

He glanced at her and shrugged out of his coat, folding it over the back of a chair. She sat in one of the chairs looking out the window where lights shone on the empty veranda. Green palm fronds waved gently in the breeze. Complementing the tall trees, beds of red, yellow and purple exotic hibiscus circled the base of each tree. The lawn ran to the sandy beach and in the distance, lights twinkled on luxury yachts.

"Attractive grounds, too. This is fantastic real estate," he said quietly. His low voice was velvety when he pulled a chair near hers and faced her. He stretched out his long legs and looked relaxed and her curiosity grew about why he wanted to see her privately.

When she crossed her tanned legs, he glanced down and then his eyes returned to hers.

She tilted her head to study him. "So you did have a reason for coming tonight, besides eating," she said.

"Nope. I came for dinner and thought I'd be back at El Diablo long before now. I got sidetracked. As for talking to you, I intended to call tomorrow and ask for an appointment. I didn't expect to meet you tonight. When I've eaten here before, I haven't seen you."

"Okay. So, here we are. You don't have to wait until tomorrow. What's this about?"

Emilio gazed at her in silence and her curiosity mounted. Whatever he intended to discuss must be serious.

"You know how rumors fly in this business," he said finally.

His words chilled her. She hoped she kept her features impassive while she looked steadily back at him, but all she could think was that there would be only one rumor that would bring a competitor from another restaurant to see her. Was her accountant's embezzlement public knowledge? A suffocating heat enveloped her. If Emilio Jefferies knew about her loss, how long before her family knew?

She reassured herself that Parker didn't know or she would have already heard from him.

"Go ahead," she said stiffly and wished she sounded more relaxed. She was thankful now that they were in dim light.

"Your accountant has disappeared."

"Yes, that's right. And since you know that much, you must know the rest of the story about him. But that isn't why you wanted to talk to me—to confirm something you could verify in other ways."

"No. Do you mind me asking if your brothers know about this?"

"No, they don't and frankly, I'm disappointed that rumors are circulating, because I'd just as soon my brothers don't know about it just yet."

"That's reasonable," Emilio said.

"So what did you want to discuss about it?" she asked, barely able to think about anything except Parker would soon know if he didn't already.

"From the rumors, I gather your accountant is not all that's missing."

"The rumors, unfortunately, are correct. My trusted accountant left with my money. This doesn't have anything to do with El Diablo, though. So what's on your mind?"

"I have a business proposition for you," Emilio answered in his deep voice.

Startled, she again hoped she didn't reveal her surprise. "I'm not selling Brittany Beach," she snapped, clenching her fists in her lap, thinking the vultures were already circling.

"That's not why I'm here," Emilio assured her with a wave of his hand. "You've been doing a bang-up job of running this."

"Then what do you want?" she asked in surprise. "If you expect me to borrow money from you—that's out, as well, because I can always go to my family."

"Ah, I don't think you will go to them," Emilio replied softly. "I'm guessing that if you were going to your ambitious brothers, you would have already gone. I have to admit that I'm surprised your brothers don't already know about your loss."

"They're preoccupied right now with settling our father's estate," she explained, recalling the reading of her father's will last month. She had no intention of telling Emilio what an incredible shock it had been to learn that her father had had a second life and they had another sibling, Cassie Sinclair, who managed the Garrison Grand Bahamas.

She wondered how much that information had circulated, suspecting everyone in the family would be reluctant to talk about it to an outsider. The discovery of the relationship had been stunning and at the time, Parker had been livid. Brittany knew even now, a month later, his attention was on the division of his power.

"Besides, as I'm sure you've heard, Parker's in love, so he's preoccupied," she added. "My other brothers are involved in the same estate issues. I think that's what's given me a reprieve from discovery." She ran her fingers along her skirt, forgetting her family and thinking about Emilio. "If you aren't offering to buy me out or loan me money, what's on your mind?" she asked.

"Quid pro quo—a trade. I cover your loss and, therefore, your brothers don't step in and take over."

Surprised, Brittany stared at him. *Cover her loss.* The words nagged at her and she knew the desperate situation she was in left her few choices. Even so, her first reaction was refusal, because she didn't want a stranger mixing into her business.

"Thank you, but I don't think that's feasible," Brittany answered politely, feeling cold that an outsider even knew about her financial crisis.

"Don't give me a hasty reply," he answered with a wave of his hand, dismissing her rejection. "Let's talk it over."

As she shook her head, he leaned forward and caught her hand, making her pulse jump with the contact. His palm was warm, gently holding hers. In spite of his caring manner, she could feel the clash of wills between them. She pulled her hand away and locked her fingers in her lap to keep from wringing her hands, which was what she wanted to do.

"Your brother Parker, as head of the umbrella corporation for all of the Garrison enterprises, has the funds to cover your loss, but I understand your reluctance to go to your family," Emilio said in a reminder that brought her worries crashing back.

"Right. They're not one of my current options," she said

stiffly, shuddering slightly at just the thought of walking into Parker's office in downtown Miami and announcing that two million had been stolen from her by her accountant. "I intend to work this out myself."

"Ah," Emilio said and satisfaction flared in his green eyes.

She hurt, knowing she was caught in a dreadful dilemma. Everything in her cried out to tell Emilio no and get him out of her office, yet her desperation held her silent. Finally, she couldn't resist asking, "You'd cover my loss. In return, what do you want?"

"A share of Brittany Beach for my investment."

Her immediate reaction was *never.* "I can't do that!"

"Think about it," he said. "You'd wipe out your loss. Your debts would be covered and gone."

Temptation tore at her. An inner voice urged her to accept and the prospects made her heart race. This was the miracle she had searched for, so why were warnings going off steadily in her mind?

"How big a share do you want?" Brittany asked, biting her lip while her mind raced. Everything in her still screamed no, yet if she didn't cover her losses, next week she had to go to Parker.

"That depends on how big my investment is," Emilio replied easily, sitting back in the chair again and watching her. He looked relaxed and sounded as casual and cool as if he were discussing the menu for breakfast. Yet his green eyes were alert and she thought again of a panther, only this time, one ready to pounce on its prey.

She hated to say the amount out loud. It was massive, impossible for her to replace by herself. Emilio waited patiently for her reply. She raised her chin as she wondered how many hundreds of times the total figure had run through her thoughts and kept her awake at night. "It's slightly over two million dollars."

He pursed his lips and sat in silence as if mulling it over.

While she was surprised by his lack of reaction to the horrific amount, she thought about her brothers. If they heard the amount, they would be wild and demanding to know why she hadn't been on top of things and known what her accountant was doing.

While Emilio remained silent, she wondered what he was thinking. She knew the loss was monumental and disappointment shook her while she braced for him to withdraw his offer.

"Two million is a sizable figure. Any hope of catching the accountant?"

"No one knows where he went," she said stiffly, and then they lapsed into silence again. Waiting, she watched as he made a triangle of his fingers and, evidently, mulled over the amount.

"Two million," he repeated. He looked at her sharply. "Do you own the building and land?"

"I own the building, but the land is part of the Garrison holdings."

He nodded. The silence became oppressive and her nerves stretched. Now that she'd had salvation dangled in front of her, she didn't want it yanked away.

"Okay. I'll cover your debts," he declared.

She let out her breath. She didn't know whether she wanted to accept or refuse, but it was a relief to know she had an option.

"So, do you have an idea how big a share of Brittany Beach you want in exchange for your investment?" she asked and then held her breath again while she waited for his answer.

Two

"If I put that much cash into Brittany Beach, I want a fifty-fifty partnership."

"Fifty-fifty?" Stunned, she hadn't expected that large a percentage, but she really hadn't thought through his offer.

She jumped to her feet and had to move and get away from his steady gaze. Her mind raced over his proposition. She crossed the room to the window to watch breakers hit the shore without really seeing them.

She would have to give up her complete control. Everything in her told her to refuse. With half control, Emilio would be in charge as much as she. She spun around to face him.

"I'd have to share everything with you—running Brittany Beach, all decisions about the restaurant?"

"You sure would," he replied quietly. "It also means that you save Brittany Beach without relying on your family to rescue you. Plus, you'll have my business experience available—the old, 'sometimes two heads are better than one' theory."

"You and I would have to work closely together every day," she said and one corner of his mouth quirked up in a crooked grin.

"Brittany, that would never be a hardship," he drawled.

His words made her pulse jump because he was flirting, yet she couldn't smile in return. She didn't want to take this man as a business partner. She knew his playboy reputation. Sexy and attractive, he disturbed her and she had a reaction to him. Until the past few minutes, she'd enjoyed the evening with him, but that was different from going into business with him.

He had a history as a heartbreaker and she didn't want to become one on the list. She liked being on her own. Another drawback was that she didn't know him. Could she trust him with fifty percent of Brittany Beach? At the same time, while doubts assailed her, his offer hung in the air like a golden salvation.

She couldn't keep from considering what he was proposing. He would cover her monstrous debt—she would not have to borrow money, pay interest and sink deeper into debt. She hoped she kept her features impassive.

"That's a generous offer," she said quietly, walking back to sit facing him. "Why are you extending your help to me? We're competitors and we don't know each other."

He smiled. "Anyone can read the press you've gotten and know you're operating a popular, hip place. You've done well. I consider half interest in Brittany Beach a good investment."

"Thank you," she replied, her mind racing over questions. "We don't know each other. Can I trust you?" she asked, looking into green eyes that were unfathomable. She couldn't guess what he was thinking. How much could she trust a handsome, wealthy playboy who broke women's hearts?

"Cold, hard cash is a good sign of trust, don't you think?" he asked with a smile.

"Yes. Two million is," she said, more to herself than to him. "I don't know if you have a violent temper or if you're a perfectionist and highly demanding," she continued, yet all the time she protested, part of her yearned to accept his offer and toss consequences to the wind. "I don't know whether your employees like working for you."

"You don't have to make this decision now," he replied. "My offer is on the table. Think it over. You can check me out and you can talk to some of my employees."

"I have to decide soon. You know the daily demands of a restaurant. We can't run on credit."

"Garrison credit? That'll sustain you for a time. If you want to know more about me, spend a day at El Diablo and watch me work. You'll get an idea of how I do things and you'll know me better."

He was making her a good offer and being reasonable about letting her check him out, which was reassuring even if she didn't feel she could take him up on his suggestions. She couldn't resist glancing at her desk, too aware of the drawer with a stack of bills that grew bigger daily. "At this point, I don't have the luxury of waiting," she answered truthfully.

"Whatever you need to do. You know my offer. Think about it."

"Frankly, it's salvation," she declared bluntly, wondering if at some point, she might be able to buy back the fifty percent. Or, if they worked well together, it would be a permanent arrangement.

"Do you have any questions?" he asked.

"How involved do you want to be in running Brittany Beach?"

"Until I know your staff and restaurant and everything about this place, I'd like to participate daily in management."

The prospect of constant, involved contact with Emilio sizzled in her. Could she work with this sexy charmer and keep her heart intact? On the business side—his offer was the answer to her prayers. In truth, she had exhausted every possibility for saving Brittany Beach.

Once again, she got up to go to the window while she thought about his offer. In four days, she would need funds that she didn't have. She could borrow enough to get by temporarily, but the moment she got a loan, word might get back to Parker. Friday to Monday.

"Brittany," Emilio said casually, and she turned to face him. "Sleep on it. Or, if it helps, I can advance you a loan while you consider my offer," he said, and that proposal in itself reassured her.

"No. Frankly, I don't have other options. I accept your offer," she replied, feeling as if her future was sealed and it would be a long time—if ever—before she would have full control of her business. She recalled an old song or perhaps a quote—something about dancing with the devil. Was that what she had agreed to? Had she sold her soul to keep her restaurant? Emilio had a reputation that rang bells of alarm the moment he walked into Brittany Beach. Yet she'd enjoyed his company tonight and he'd been reasonable in making his offer and had not pressured her to accept. Besides, the instant she uttered acceptance, an enormous burden had lifted from her shoulders.

"Awesome!" he exclaimed, standing and striding around the desk while he flashed another brilliant, irresistible smile at her that banished her dark thoughts. His contagious enthusiasm made her feel she had made a fabulous choice.

He placed his hands lightly on her shoulders. "Fantastic! This bargain will be great, and you'll keep your restaurant."

"I'll share Brittany Beach with you, is what you mean," she replied, gazing up at him. He was only inches away. His jaw was clean-shaven, his lower lip full and sensual. She could detect his aftershave and was aware of the warmth of his hands through her silk blouse. He was easily the most handsome man she had known and it scared her to think about trying to overlook his appeal and work with him daily.

"My guess is, that we'll have more women customers now," she remarked drily and received another flash of white, even teeth while his eyes sparkled.

"I think I noticed more male customers out there tonight than female."

"It won't be that way for long."

"Don't sound so unhappy about it. If you change your mind tonight, let me know. This deal isn't consummated yet," he said, watching her closely.

Relieved to hear him make such a statement, she nodded. "I guess I'm panicking because I'm giving up part of Brittany Beach."

"Don't look at what you're losing. Remember what you're gaining—Brittany Beach. Plus, an experienced business partner," he added with another engaging grin that again reminded her why females were so drawn to him. She couldn't resist smiling in return.

"How could I question such a deal?" she asked.

"Good! Now you don't look quite like you've agreed for the world to disintegrate."

Her smile broadened. "This has happened so fast. I need to get used to the changes that are coming."

"I predict we'll make more money together than ever," he said in his gravelly, deep voice. "You'll see," he added, squeezing her shoulders and then releasing her to place his hands on his hips. "So how about getting together in the morning to draw up a contract?"

"We're moving fast. Morning is fine."

"We'll go only as fast as you want to go," he said. "I promise. Let me know if you're unhappy."

She nodded again, reassured by each of his statements and hoping he meant what he said.

"At any time until we sign the contract and money is deposited, you can back out of our deal and it's fine. Once we sign a contract, I want to know that I have a lasting agreement. Okay with you?"

"That's fair enough," she replied, unable to smile or display the enthusiasm he obviously felt. Yet she thought he was being more than fair with her.

"As soon as we sign our agreement, I'll deposit the money into your account, and then we'll be in business. From what you said, you have to move swiftly on this."

"Yes, I do," she said, once again thinking about her family and how long before word reached them. Would they have a fit over her taking Emilio as a partner? She was certain any dislike of her new partner would pale in comparison to their reaction if they knew about her loss of money.

"So how about nine in the morning for the two of us to look at a contract tomorrow before we meet with our lawyers?" Emilio asked.

"Let me check my calendar," she said, walking to her desk while he followed and stood close beside her. "Nine o'clock will be fine with me."

"If it's possible, let's get together in the afternoon—you, me and our attorneys."

"I'll try to make an afternoon appointment with my lawyer and you contact yours. I'll use our family attorney," she said as she thought about Brandon Washington, their tall, capable lawyer "He'll be bound by attorney-client confidentiality and I trust Brandon. In the long run, it'll be better to have him because he knows about my business."

"Sure. If I tell mine it's urgent, he'll try to rearrange his schedule."

"Let me give you my attorney's card," she said, opening her desk and reaching for one, which she handed to Emilio. She stepped back slightly, realizing he stood only inches away. Amusement danced in his eyes.

"I don't bite. Might like to, though," he said.

Laughing, she shook her finger at him. She pulled out another card and wrote on the back of it. "There's my card with my cell phone and my home phone."

"If we're exchanging personal numbers, I'll give you mine," he said, pulling out a billfold to get one of his cards. He picked up a pen from her desk and scrawled his numbers and while his head was bent, she looked at his thick, black hair. He glanced up and she drew a deep breath, knowing he had caught her studying him. He handed the card to her and she dropped it on her desk.

"Perhaps it would be wiser to have the meeting at your lawyer's office. I don't care to run into one of my brothers at Brandon's office," she said.

"Good idea," Emilio replied.

She bit her lower lip. "There's something else I'd like to do," she said. "For the time being, can we keep this partnership out of the news?"

He shrugged one broad shoulder. "I suppose."

"It's not you," she said quickly. "It's my family. If we don't make an official announcement, there will be less chance of knowledge of the embezzlement getting back to my family. I've told you, I prefer to work this partnership and Brittany Beach finances out myself."

"I understand about family. They're the best, but sometimes, you want them to let you manage your life without suggestions. If we don't make a public announcement right now, it's okay with me," he said easily, his eyes wide and guileless. "What will you tell your staff, because I'll be here daily?"

While she pondered his question, she focused on a point behind him. "How about simply saying that you're doing some consulting for me, that you're lending your business expertise?"

"That's fine with me," he replied, smiling at her. He tilted up her chin and her pulse accelerated. "See, we can work together."

"At least for five minutes," she remarked, knowing she sounded negative. "I'm still sorting through this and getting accustomed to the idea of a partner."

"I'll remind you again. Get used to the notion of no debt. For your part, that's the big deal and what you want. And remember, tonight, you can still back out."

"You're too good to be true," she replied, wondering about him and if she needed to take the weekend to think over his offer.

"No, I'm not. I'm in the same business and I have money to invest and this looks like a super opportunity. We're going to be great together," he said in a husky voice that instantly removed all thoughts of business from her mind. He smiled. "This partnership will be terrific."

"I'll remind you of that remark when we have the first fight," she replied.

"A fight with you—never!" he exclaimed emphatically as his gaze lowered to her mouth and made her heart miss a beat. "We'll just do things my way," he teased with another charming grin.

"You think I'm going to give in to your every whim?" she asked in a seductive drawl and something flickered in the depths of his eyes as his smile vanished. She knew she shouldn't flirt with him, but it was impossible to resist.

"If I could have one wish—" he began, but she interrupted him.

She shook her head. "If you could have one wish, it would not be that I would yield to your whims! SoBe is filled with really gorgeous, sexy women who will yield to what you want eagerly. I think you flirt out of habit, but I've seen pictures of you too many times and the woman at your side is always drop-dead gorgeous and often a star or famous in another field."

"You don't have to take a backseat to any of them," he said softly as he studied her features.

She laughed. "So compliments come with this deal?"

"Only if deserved," he retorted.

"We've got business to transact, remember?"

"My practical partner," he teased, running his index finger lightly along her cheek and making her pulse flutter.

With an effort, she walked away from him, circling her desk and then turning to face him. "We can make an official announcement about the partnership later, when things are running smoothly. We can have the public celebration and the fanfare."

Emilio placed his hands on his hips again. "I don't need fanfare. I'm satisfied with the bargain we'll make. We'll be an awesome team. This is great, Brittany."

"I hope so," she said.

"Remember, no debt. Hold on to that."

"I'll try," she said,

"I'll go now," he said, turning toward the door and pocketing her card.

"I'll walk with you to the front," she said, hurrying to catch up to him at the door.

He held open the door for her and she left her office feeling as if the past hour had changed her life forever and she would never again be the same.

"Tomorrow morning we can go over what we need in a contract and I'm sure our attorneys will have suggestions. I have a boilerplate contract we can use," he said, but she could barely keep her mind on what he was telling her as she walked beside him and thought about the commitment she had just made. Emilio Jefferies was her new partner.

How long would it take her to get accustomed to that? Probably not long because she was certain he would make his presence felt.

At the front, she stood with him while he waited for a valet to bring his car.

"See you tomorrow," he said. He gave her one last smile before he went striding to his car. She didn't wait to watch him drive away, but hurried back to her office to close the door.

She wished Emilio would turn all management over to her, but she could understand. If she invested in his restaurant, she would want to be involved in running it, too.

Emilio—her partner. The idea of working constantly in close contact with him created a honeyed warmth. In every move and tone and look, Emilio was seductive and it had been exhilarating to flirt with him early in the evening before they got into something serious.

She flung her arms out. "Here's to success, my new partnership and to saving Brittany Beach!" she exclaimed to the empty office. Her relief was enormous. And he had left her an out, which reassured her each time she thought about it.

She hurried around the desk and sat to phone the family lawyer and make an appointment.

Within minutes, Brandon Washington agreed to get in touch with Emilio's attorney and set a time for an appointment. It was an hour before schedules were adjusted and they had an appointment for two in the afternoon the next day.

The sooner the money was deposited in her business account, the sooner she would be safe from discovery about the embezzlement.

She opened her lower desk drawer and surveyed the stack of bills that had accumulated. Now she could pay them!

Brittany glanced at her watch and called Boyd Dumont, the

accountant who had audited the books and found the embezzlement, to tell him her news.

After she had told Boyd goodbye, she made a list of things to do. The phone rang and her pulse jumped when she heard Emilio's deep voice. He told her that he wanted to talk so they could get to know each other a little better and asked her what time she'd go home.

Smiling, she leaned back in her chair and told him shortly after one. He said he'd call her then.

Wanting to finish at the office and get home, she replaced the receiver. Emilio had flirted, charmed her and then made the fantastic offer. Thinking about talking to him later, she hummed as she turned back to her list. While she was writing, someone knocked on her door.

"Come in," Brittany called, and her director of services thrust his head inside.

"We have an actor and his party and he's agreed to pictures. I thought you might like to meet him and be in the pictures."

"Of course," she said, knowing this was good publicity for Brittany Beach. She got up and smoothed her red skirt, and left with Hector.

It was almost one in the morning when Brittany entered her two-bedroom condo on the ground floor in an exclusive SoBe gated area. Always happy to be home, she welcomed the quiet after the busy restaurant.

Overlooking the ocean, the living room held her books and favorite Jasper Johns paintings, and after her shower, she played Otis Redding, turning the music low, enjoying it and realizing that she felt relaxed for the first time since the discovery of the embezzlement.

Wondering what to wear tomorrow, she entered her closet and looked at possibilities, selecting a white linen suit with a deep-blue silk blouse.

She held the suit up in front of her as she looked at herself in the mirror, but she was seeing Emilio. She liked him. Tonight it had been exhilarating to flirt with him and enjoyable to talk to him. And she felt a hot physical reaction that she thought he'd experienced, too. She laughed out loud at herself over that one! Emilio probably had the same reaction with every female he encountered. Handsome and sexy, he was one of those men whom women loved. She would have no doubt about that, even if she hadn't seen a multitude of press articles about him buzzing around SoBe escorting socialites or stars. "You better keep your wits with him," she told herself aloud.

Then her phone rang. Eagerly, she plopped on her bed and listened to Emilio's hello.

When she finally told him good night, they had talked over an hour. Afterward, while she tried to go to sleep, she thought about his call. They had talked about favorite things, the newest SoBe restaurant, restaurant menus. Jumping from topic to topic, she'd enjoyed their conversation and she looked forward to seeing him again. Maybe this partnership would be as great as he predicted.

The next hours were restless. She dreamed about Emilio, once waking with thoughts of him still in her mind, drifting asleep again until later, when her eyes flew open and she stared into the darkness as a chill shook her.

Glancing around to see it was almost five in the morning, Brittany sat up while fears and doubts bombarded her. Had she rushed to take a partner too swiftly? Had she once again been too trusting? Emilio had come to her with his offer. Did he have an ulterior motive and, if he did, what was it?

Tossing back the sheet, she paced the floor. With every doubt that assailed her, she reminded herself of her dilemma that had had no solution until Emilio. She repeatedly thought about his promise that she could back out of the deal until they had signed the contract. He had been willing to give her time, to let her investigate him, to let her call the whole thing off. With offers like the ones he'd made, how could he have ulterior motives?

Three

By the time of their appointment the next morning, Brittany had spent an hour going over details for the coming day at Brittany Beach. She was in the main dining room when she looked up to see someone ushering Emilio in her direction. At the sight of him, her pulse jumped. This morning he was dressed in a charcoal business suit and red tie with his snowy shirt.

She had already talked to him twice on the telephone this morning. Over and over she wondered if they could work out an agreement by early afternoon. The speed they were moving astounded her. She finished what she was doing, handed the approved menus to her sous-chef and walked forward to meet Emilio.

"Good morning." She greeted him with a smile as she extended her hand.

"Good morning," he replied, warm appreciation in his eyes as they drifted over her white skirt and blue blouse, down to her peep-toe white pumps with stiletto heels. "You look great."

"Thank you," she said, aware of his hand wrapped around hers. His hand was brown, warm, his fingers well-shaped and his touch stirred a fiery tingle.

"Let's go back to my office. I'll send for coffee," she said.

She motioned him to sit at the table. In minutes, a staff person brought a tray with coffee, tea and orange juice, along with glasses and white china cups and saucers.

When Brittany sat, Emilio moved his chair beside her. "I brought the boilerplate contract," he said, opening his briefcase and removing two copies. When he handed a copy to her, his hand barely brushed hers. Each contact was volatile, and she wondered how long she would continue to have such an intense reaction to him. How was she going to work in close proximity to him if she couldn't control her response to everything he did? When would she view him as ordinary and not get that tingle if he casually brushed against her? She drew a deep breath and turned to focus on the contract.

Emilio pointed to the first paragraph and read aloud. It was an effort to concentrate on business with only inches separating them. She should put a foot of space between them, but she didn't want him to realize his effect on her.

They slowly went through the agreements and stipulations and she stared at the paragraph that gave him fifty percent ownership of Brittany Beach. Once she signed the contract there would be no turning back.

When she signed the papers, though, her debt would be wiped out. Whenever doubts loomed, she reminded herself of what was at stake and what she was getting. Solvency.

She was surprised how swiftly and cooperatively they worked out the details.

By noon, she sat back and confessed, "That went smoother than I expected."

"I agree," Emilio said. "That's another good indicator that we'll work together well."

She had already ordered lunch from the kitchen and they had it delivered to the veranda outside her office.

As she stirred lemon into her chilled glass of iced tea, Brittany's spirits rose another notch. "I have a recent picture of our staff that I'll give you after lunch. Most everyone is in it and their names are printed below. I'll introduce you to as many as I can, but I don't want to have a formal meeting and introduction because it'll make a bigger deal about you being here."

"Sounds okay to me," he said, smiling at her.

She made a notation in a tablet beside her plate. He leaned forward. "You're still working. Let it go through lunch. Tonight, let's have an official celebration at El Diablo. Come join me for dinner," he suggested.

Warnings went off in her thoughts like sirens in a storm. The man was a heartthrob, she reminded herself at the same moment she nodded her head.

"Against good judgment, I accept."

"Against good judgment," he repeated. "Now how do you figure that?" he asked, a dark eyebrow arching.

"I suspect you're a heartbreaker and I definitely think work and fun should be separate."

"Nonsense on both charges. We're sensible enough to mix business and pleasure, and since when isn't that mixed all over SoBe? As for the heartbreaker accusation—I don't think so. I can't recall any teary-eyed ladies languishing in my past," he said with a twinkle in his green eyes.

"Your memory may be poor on the subject."

"Let's celebrate an event that will be mutually profitable. How can you avoid being elated over the future possibilities?"

"I'm happy about it," she said, gazing into his compelling eyes and thinking about her quiet life.

He laughed. "You sound as if you're headed for a disaster. But you said yes, so we're on for tonight. Maybe I can cheer you up."

She smiled. "It's not that bad. I'm trying to get used to what's happening here."

"Get accustomed to me," he said softly. "I'm here to stay."

She laughed and he nodded. "That's better. This is good, Brittany. You'll see."

She felt better and her worries diminished slightly. In spite of his denial, she couldn't imagine that her assessment of him wasn't right on target. Yet she couldn't resist the prospect of the celebration. She shoved away the tablet and placed her pen on the table.

"Very well. I'll put away my list for now. But I do want to say that after we finish eating, let's look around to see about an office for you. We really don't have an extra one that is the size you need."

"Show me what you do have. I don't need anything large."

"Is it going to be a hardship for you to divide your time between your restaurant and this one?"

As he shook his head, wind caught locks of his black hair, lifting them slightly away from his face. His wavy midnight hair was as thick and appealing as his other features. She realized she was staring at him and looked away.

"I have excellent people who can manage El Diablo," he replied. "At first, I want to familiarize myself with your staff and your procedures. I'd like to get to know your regular clientele—which do you have the highest percentage of, regulars or single visits?"

"Both, maybe equally. We're getting celebrities, models, jet-setters—they all generate publicity."

They sat beneath a large blue umbrella, so they were shaded from direct sunlight, but they were outside where the light was strong and Emilio's thickly lashed eyes looked like clear-green glass except, unlike glass, there was a fire in the depths of his gaze that kept her pulse fluttering.

As they talked about trivial matters, Emilio was the one who brought up her family. "I'm sorry you lost your father."

"Thank you. When I was growing up, he seemed powerful and invincible and there's still a part of me that's shocked by his death."

"I think that's natural. Do you see your siblings often?"

"Yes, I do. We try to have a family gathering for Sunday night dinner and we see each other often during the week. What about your family?"

"My brother, Jordan, and I see each other daily. We're the last ones left in our immediate family."

"That's good. There's a lot of sibling rivalry in my family," she said.

"I'll introduce you the first time I have a chance," Emilio replied. Brittany remembered hearing that Emilio's mother came to America from Cuba when he was an infant and she became the Jefferies' nanny. When she was killed, Emilio was adopted by the Jefferies.

"Does Jordan know about your new partnership?"

"Not yet," Emilio replied, "but simply because I haven't had the opportunity to tell him. The first chance I get, I'll let him know. I'll also tell him we're keeping it private for now."

"It'll be more acceptable if it's business as usual when I let my family know. I can't see how they can object to what I want to do with the restaurant as long as it's growing and profitable." She glanced at Emilio's empty glass. "More tea? Would you like anything else to eat or drink?"

"No, thanks."

"Then lunch is over and we can get back to business. Let me show you the offices and after we decide what we'll do about yours, we'll tour the entire restaurant."

Soon the time approached to leave for their appointment with the lawyers. Brittany stopped in her office to comb her hair, once again fastening it up in a clip. She pulled on a cropped, white linen jacket that matched her skirt, pushing up the sleeves and glancing at herself in the mirror before leaving to meet Emilio.

As she walked up to him, she saw the approval in his eyes when he looked at her warmly. "This has to be the best deal I've ever made," he said in a husky voice, taking her arm.

"Don't turn on the charm. We're business partners."

"That doesn't keep me from appreciating a beautiful woman," he replied and smiled at her while he leaned down to open the car door.

It took the entire afternoon to iron out the details they wanted in the contract. Finally, the moment came when she watched Emilio write the check and her heart thudded at the amount, even though she had known exactly what it would be. Relief surged, making her hands clammy. She fought the urge to reach out for the check before he was ready to give it to her.

He held it out. "Here's the money. We need to get it transferred to your account from mine. As soon as we finish here, we'll go to your bank."

With cold fingers, she took the check that meant even more now than when her father had first given her the papers for Brittany Beach. "Thank you," she exclaimed, squeezing his hand.

His eyebrow arched, and she realized he might have misinterpreted her gesture of gratitude for something more. Dismissing the notion, she put the check into her purse.

She realized he must have been certain about her decision to accept his offer because he had everything ready to move instantly, and the notion that he anticipated all this happening raised another flag of warning deep inside her.

She shrugged away the worry. She had no choice, and this partnership would save Brittany Beach.

At half past five they had a brief meeting with her new accountant.

It was almost seven when they finally finished and Emilio pulled up in front of Brittany Beach. "Sure you don't want me to pick you up tonight?"

"Positive. It's not that far and I'll drive myself over."

"See you at half past nine," Emilio said. "I'm looking forward to our dinner. No business whatsoever tonight. This will be pure celebration."

She smiled. "You know the old saying, 'All play and no work makes Jack a lazy bum,'" she said, and his smile widened.

"You made that up."

"I might have," she admitted, grinning at him.

"I think you need to learn how to let go and enjoy yourself."

"I know how to let go," she replied. "You'll see. I can have fun."

"Be ready to have some tonight," he said. "When people come to El Diablo, I want them to have a good time and great food. I definitely want my new partner to."

"See you after nine," she said. She climbed out of the car and walked toward the door, glancing back over her shoulder to find him watching her. She waved and as she went inside, she heard him drive away.

Glancing briefly across the strip of beach at the blue ocean which paralleled the highway, Emilio sped back to El Diablo, sweeping into the drive and circling the exclusive pink stucco restaurant to park near his private entrance. As he turned the back corner, he saw his tall, blond, blue-eyed brother, Jordan, striding to his own car.

When Emilio waved, Jordan turned and approached.

"When I called, they said they expected you, so I stopped by and then found you weren't here," Jordan said. Wind blew locks of his thick blond hair. His open-throat blue cotton shirt clung to his muscular biceps and broad shoulders. He waved a folder at Emilio. "I need your signature on papers to open another account for Hotel Victoria. I want a separate account for the insurance."

"Sure. I want to talk to you, anyway," Emilio replied.

When they entered Emilio's quiet office, he sat behind his broad granite-and-bronze desk while Jordan sat in one of the blue leather chairs.

"Give me the papers." While Jordan waited quietly, Emilio took the folder from him and scanned the contents. He signed each paper where he was supposed to and then passed the folder back to his brother. "There. You can pay your insurance," he said cheerfully. "How's it coming with the hotel?"

Jordan shrugged. "Fine. We're approaching the opening— and looking to giving the Garrison Grand some real competition with our luxury hotel."

"It's not as big as the Garrison, but it's opulent and should draw the same jet-set crowd. So everything is going all right?"

"A shipment of furniture was delivered to the wrong hotel," Jordan answered, shrugging one broad shoulder. "Other than minor blips, we're sailing along great."

Emilio smiled. "You'll get it all worked out. You're still on schedule, aren't you?"

"Yep. Why did you want to see me?" Jordan asked.

"Remember I told you that I've heard all sorts of gossip from my staff and restaurant friends about Brittany Beach?"

"Yeah, that the accountant disappeared with embezzled millions. The restaurant would be on the auction block soon. The oldest Garrison was taking over. Why? Is any of it true?" Jordan asked.

"I thought there was enough to assume some of the speculation was true, so I ate dinner there and checked it out. The accountant disappeared and money's gone."

"Theft won't slow the Garrisons. They'll replace the money, put the accountant in jail and go on with business as usual."

"Not quite. Remember, Brittany Beach is Brittany Garrison's baby," Emilio said.

Jordan shrugged. "That doesn't matter. Her brothers will step in immediately."

"That's what I figured, but they haven't. They don't know what's happened and Brittany doesn't want them knowing."

Jordan smiled. "Of course, she doesn't because she doesn't want them taking the place away from her."

"I've made her a business proposition," Emilio said. He looked at his brother who was ruthlessly ambitious. "I agreed to pay her debt."

"The hell you did!" Jordan sat up straighter and his eyes narrowed. "What are you getting in exchange?"

"Half of Brittany Beach," Emilio announced triumphantly and was pleased at the sudden flare of approval in Jordan's eyes, but then it was gone as he scowled at Emilio.

"It's the Garrisons' business. They'll never let you get control or take it away from them."

Emilio leaned forward. "The Garrison men don't know it. Brittany and I drew up the contract with our lawyers this afternoon and we signed it. It's a done deal. I now have half of Brittany Beach, and there isn't one thing the Garrisons can do about this transaction."

"I'll be damned!" Jordan exclaimed, staring at Emilio. "Half! Good for you! Congratulations! We own Garrison property! I'm shocked. Doesn't she know we're at war with her brothers?"

"No," Emilio said flatly. "If she had a clue what goes on with her brothers, she wouldn't have responded the way she did. They probably tell her nothing."

Jordan whistled. "How could she not know? Half of SoBe knows what a feud we have with the Garrisons."

"Believe me, she's as naive and trusting as a lamb. She wants to keep this merger quiet, for the time being, until everything is in place and running smoothly. She's telling her employees that I'm a consultant."

Jordan's eyes narrowed. "How much money?"

"Slightly over two million," Emilio answered.

Jordan whistled. "Wow, again. The guy embezzled two million bucks and she didn't know it?"

"She's a baby. I don't know what her twin is like, but they're the babies of that family and Brittany really is one. No doubt a little princess whose daddy tossed this restaurant to her. I walked in there with my proposition, and she accepted it with relief. From the first minute she trusted me."

"Awesome!"

"Jordan, listen," Emilio urged, leaning forward. "Give me time and we'll own all of it. Do you know what a coup that will be? Taking it right out from under the Garrisons. I can see how her accountant waltzed off with her money. She doesn't have business judgment or this embezzlement wouldn't have ever happened. I know I can take Brittany Beach away from her," he repeated. "Give me time."

"Won't that be something! When that happens, Parker and Stephen will go up in flames," Jordan said with a grin. "When the Garrison men learn you own half, they may be ready to yank her out of there and sell you the other half, solely to end a Garrison-Jefferies partnership."

"We'll see how it plays out, but I'm sure I'll get the restaurant."

"That's sweet, Emilio." Jordan stood and tapped the folder against his knee. "I need to be in downtown Miami soon, so I'll take my papers and go. Keep me posted."

As soon as the door shut behind Jordan, Emilio turned to gaze outside while visions of Brittany crowded out other thoughts.

Brittany was an appealing woman, sexy, stirring him easily.

They had a volatile chemistry between them and even though she tried to focus on business, he knew she felt the sparks, too.

He recalled in exact detail the moment he had glanced across her dining room and seen her looking at him. Her fiery-red skirt and red silk blouse had been an invitation. Her long shapely legs were as fabulous as her tiny waist and lush, full breasts.

Thinking about Brittany, Emilio was getting aroused.

She was good-looking and he had enjoyed her company and talking to her. That was a bonus he'd never figured on. He turned to pick up the phone and give her a call.

The minute she answered and he said hello, he leaned back in his chair to prop his feet on his desk. "I wanted to see if you're still happy and if you're looking forward to dinner tonight," he said, nodding over her answer. Twenty minutes passed before she had to go and he replaced his receiver, more eager than ever to see her again tonight. He drummed his fingers restlessly on his desk while he thought about dinner and what he wanted. Anticipation made him eager.

Whistling a tune, he looked around his own office that was a contrast to Brittany's teak and glass and hardwood floor. He had a white marble floor, white walls and a granite desk. There were accents of bright primary colors on his walls in his contemporary art. Deep-blue cushions and blue pots holding palms added more color.

His gaze rested on a particular painting he owned. He looked at the bright colors and abstract shapes by a new artist named Richardson, while he wondered if Brittany would recognize it and remember when he had outbid her for the picture. At the time, they hadn't met and he wondered if she would even recall the incident. If she did, she was going to be less than happy with him about it.

His office was large and luxurious, but he didn't care what kind of office he had at Brittany Beach. He just wanted the fifty percent control that he now had. He'd launched the Jefferies' invasion of the Garrison properties. And he'd acquired a gorgeous partner.

Again, his blood heated when he thought about her and he stood restlessly. He yanked open a top drawer and grabbed up a handful of photos and tossed them on his desk, spreading them with his fingers. The pictures were shots of Brittany Beach, taken last week. A rush of satisfaction surged in him as he picked up one particular picture. Brittany stood in front of the restaurant, talking to a nondescript man who held a rake and Emilio assumed the man was a gardener. Brittany wore a diaphanous skirt and open top with a skimpy blue slash of silk across her breasts. The filmy skirt rode low on her hips and beneath it she wore electric-blue shorts that were as skimpy as her matching top. For a woman who was cautious about love, her wardrobe screamed seduction and sensuality. He smiled and ran his finger over her picture, remembering the sparks that sizzled between them. He scooped up the pictures to drop them back into his drawer as he decided he would have Brittany and her restaurant, too.

He headed toward his kitchen to make plans for the evening. When he strode through his main dining room, he glanced around at his own restaurant with its ambience of seduction. Tonight, pink and rose lighting would give a heightened sensuality to the platforms that contained beds for dining. His pulse jumped at the thought of being with Brittany and he glanced at his watch, counting the minutes until it was time for her arrival.

Shortly after eight in the evening, Brittany returned to her condo to get ready for dinner with Emilio. Anticipation bubbled in her. Ignoring worries, she bathed and selected a black sheath dress that ended above her knees. Black stiletto T-strap pumps added to her height.

As she dressed, she listened to the weather report. A hurricane was far out in the Atlantic, but it was on a westward course. In seconds, her thoughts had jumped back to Emilio and she lost all interest in weather, but she'd heard enough to know the storm wouldn't make landfall until Sunday night or Monday. By that time, Brittany knew the storm could change course or dissipate.

With care, she brushed her long hair, pulling it high on one side of her head to catch it up with pins and a clip. Diamond stud earrings were her only jewelry. Finally, she picked up her small, metallic black bag and left.

Beneath a huge red neon sign that proclaimed El Diablo, a drive curved to the front door. As she circled around, she looked at lights splashing over the hot pink restaurant. Beds of exotic red flowers bloomed and lights bathed tall, graceful palms that spilled dark shadows across the green lawn. She stopped in front of the entrance, turning the key over to a valet.

Music played outside and the place was already crowded. When she entered, she crossed to the maître d', to ask for Emilio. While she waited, she looked around. Red flames were painted on hot pink walls in the entrance, highlighted by red-and-orange lighting spilling over the area. Potted palms, banana trees and tropical foliage added touches of green.

"Welcome," came a deep voice behind her and she turned to face Emilio, who smiled as his admiring regard drifted leisurely over her and he reached out to take her arm. "You look beautiful!" he said softly.

The moment she heard his voice her pulse jumped. His handsome looks were heightened by a dark gray shirt that was tucked into gray slacks.

"Thank you," she answered breathlessly, thinking each time they were together her reaction to him intensified.

"Come with me," he said. "We have a private room." He led her through part of the main dining room. "I thought you might want to see all of El Diablo."

"I've eaten here before," she said, glancing around at the beds on raised platforms. Sheer curtains were tied back, or for some, had been loosened to lend a semblance of privacy. Like decadent sultans, people lounged on beds while they partied and ate. One end of the room held a dance floor where couples gyrated to a fast beat. The noise level was high with music and laughter and conversation mingling together. "Food here has always been delicious," she added.

"I hope you were here either because of business, or with a party."

She arched her brows. "You guessed correctly in both cases," she said and his smile broadened. He took her to his kitchen and introduced her to his executive chef, a tall brown-haired man who talked briefly about the night's specialties and his favorite dishes.

As they left the kitchen, Emilio introduced her to his manager. The short blond shook hands with Brittany and welcomed her to El Diablo.

Next, Emilio led her along a hall to a room with a glass door and glass walls. Beyond it was an inner office.

"This is the reception area for my office. I want you to see my office," he said, leading her through another door and switching on a light.

As she looked around, she thought his white office with deep blue accents was as striking as the ocean view through a glass wall. "It's beautiful," she remarked, circling the room as he had done in her office. She paused in front of an abstract oil painting. "The Richardson. This is a new artist and this picture has a story behind it." She glanced over her shoulder at him.

"So you remember," he said, looking chagrined.

"How could I forget you taking this away from me?" she answered noncommittally.

"We hadn't been introduced at that time and when I did meet

you it was much later and, frankly, I hoped you'd forgotten all about the auction."

"Oh, no!" she exclaimed, remembering clearly their contest over the painting as the bidding had climbed and everyone else had dropped out. "You have good taste in art."

"At some point, I wondered if you were bidding it higher out of spite," he said.

She turned and spoke frankly. "I wanted it and I was annoyed that you continued to bid. No, I would have been happy to get it. It's still one of my favorites and I think someday, this artist will be in demand. You made a good investment, although it was crummy of you to keep bidding."

Emilio strolled over to her, standing only inches away and her pulse jumped. "Not one bit worse than your refusal to quit. So you really wanted it?"

"I wouldn't have kept bidding, otherwise, but now I suspect you must have continued because you didn't want to lose. Your suspicions of my motives indicate you took the price higher to keep someone else from besting you."

A smile hovered in his expression as he shrugged one broad shoulder and touched her cheek teasingly. "That might have been part of my reason. It's not often I get to compete with a beautiful woman."

"Thank you for the compliment. I suspect you go into all contests planning to win."

"There's no point in doing something to lose, is there?" he asked softly, and she could feel a challenge running beneath their words. Once again, she wondered how much he would interfere with her running of Brittany Beach.

She raised her chin defiantly and shot him a look that let him know she was a worthy adversary.

She saw a flicker in the depths of his eyes that she'd seen before. It was irresistible to flirt with him.

"You've made my day by joining me tonight," he said in a husky voice that stirred a tingle in her.

"No, I made your day when I signed over half my restaurant this afternoon," she retorted and he laughed.

"Maybe that, too, but tonight equals this afternoon."

"I know better than that," she teased and turned to look at the picture again. "No, I won't ever forget our bidding. I knew who you were. You didn't know me."

"I didn't, but I found out as soon as the bidding was over. After all, I had to know who my gorgeous competitor was. I meant to get over and meet you, but you slipped out of there. Afterward, when we finally did meet, because of the outcome, I didn't think it wise to bring up the auction. Frankly, I figured you'd forgotten."

"Not in this lifetime."

"So, I'm not the only one who doesn't like to lose. I'll remember that."

"Which is sort of a given that we're going to clash," she said, strolling to look at another painting. He stayed where he was and when she glanced back at him, she found him studying her.

"Hopefully, our skirmishes will be as stimulating as that one was."

"You found it invigorating because you won. I found it annoying enough to never forget about it."

"I'll have to make amends some way," he said. "Perhaps I should let you win the next contest."

"Sure, you do that," she said, finishing her tour of his office and turning toward him.

"You sound as if you think it's impossible for me to give up getting my way."

"We'll see. Actions speak louder than words."

He walked up to her and spread his palm in the center of her back. "I don't think we're going to clash in every area," he said in a deep voice and she tingled again and hoped he didn't detect her racing pulse. His mouth was well shaped, his full lower lip was sensual. What would it be like to kiss him? She suspected his kisses would be fiery and as irresistible as everything else about him. Realizing her train of thought, she looked up into a mocking expression in his green eyes. "I'm sure we're not," he added. "We'll find out."

"Eventually," she added, knowing he wasn't referring to auctions or business.

He dropped his hand. "Come along and I'll show you where we'll eat tonight."

"El Diablo looks packed already," she said as they left his office and entered the hall. "People are waiting."

"The weekends always hold capacity crowds. You have to call at least a month in advance to get a reservation," he said, opening another door and stepping back to usher her into a room that was a backdrop for seduction. "Welcome to my private dining room," he said.

Four

"Oh, my!" she exclaimed, laughing. "This is more decadent than in the main dining room," she said.

"Only as decadent as we make it," he retorted with a twinkle in his green eyes.

She shook her head. "Don't get your hopes up," she rejoined firmly.

"That's impossible. You can't imagine how high my hopes are," he said, and she laughed again. Brittany knew she shouldn't be surprised that he was good company.

"In that case, I can tell you that you're in for a letdown tonight."

"Never with you," he drawled. "So far, the evening has started out even better than I expected."

She smiled at him. "I have to agree," she said softly, and he inhaled, his chest expanding. She enjoyed sparring with him too much, even if she was crossing a line. Their light banter left business in the dust and took their relationship in a whole different direction. She felt bubbly with him, challenged and charmed.

"That gives me great hope," he said in a husky voice. "This partnership dazzles me."

"Don't pour it on. This dining room is enough," she added drily, staring at the space.

Soft-red light filled the circular room that was centered with a round bed on a raised platform. Green plants formed a backdrop along one wall. Inviting yellow cushions and pillows were propped against a low wall that surrounded half the bed area. A spread of delectable-looking yellow-and-white cheeses, bright-red strawberries, green kiwi and other tempting snacks were already on a table in the center of the bed.

"Come on, enjoy dining like a sheik," he said, offering her his hand as he kicked off his shoes.

"I thought your dining room was racy. This absolutely screams seduction."

"Ah, then it's doing what it's supposed to," he teased with a gleam in his gaze.

"Not tonight, my dear partner."

"I'll cling to that 'dear.'"

"I suspect you're accustomed to a more intimate endearment. I don't think you'll pay attention long," she said as she removed her shoes and took his hand to crawl onto the bed. His warm fingers wrapped around her hand and she looked into his eyes. The moment became electric and she drew a deep breath.

With an effort, she glanced away and climbed onto the bed, scooting to keep a distance between them. Propping herself against the pillows, she tucked her long legs beneath her and smiled at him. "Soft, red lighting. We're in bed together with champagne on ice. This promises to be an unforgettable evening, but remember, this is a business deal. View me the same as you would if it were one of my brothers who was your new partner."

"That's totally impossible," Emilio answered. "When we're alone and you're only a few feet away, I'm aware that it's you I'm with. And I've looked forward to this time all day. We have a deal to celebrate. Let go, Brittany. Stop being the businesswoman for a few hours," he coaxed.

"I think I stopped being the corporate woman when I got dressed for tonight."

Emilio stood to open the bottle of champagne that was on ice. She watched as he popped the cork, poured the golden liquid and handed her a flute. He sat beside her again and raised his glass. "Here's to a great partnership."

She touched her flute to his and took a sip of the bubbly drink. "I'm looking forward to this. Scared, too, I'll admit."

"Scared? Of me? Never!" he exclaimed. "Why would you be scared?"

"I gave up full control today. That's always scary."

"You'll see, this partnership is going to be awesome. Anytime you're unhappy, promise you'll let me know."

She smiled. "I don't think you need to worry about not knowing if I'm unhappy."

"Does this mean my partner has a temper?"

"I don't call it that," she responded. "What about you?"

"Not ever with you. That would be impossible."

"Don't make rash statements. You said you've had your fights with your brother, so there's a temper."

"Brothers have a way of provoking each other. We're close, but we both know that we're competitive and since we're the same age, we're bound to have clashes."

"Sounds as if I'm describing my life with my twin, Brooke," Brittany remarked.

Her gaze lowered to his full, sensual lips that made her pulse beat faster. It had barely been twenty-four hours since she had met and talked to him in her restaurant and here she was stretched out beside him in a bed and locked into partnership with him.

"Here's to a spectacular future for Brittany Beach," he said, lifting his glass in a toast.

She smiled as she touched her glass to his and sipped again. "So now you have El Diablo, which is successful, and you have part interest in Brittany Beach, which is growing. What are your long-range plans?"

He shrugged. "I think these two places will keep me busy. My brother and I work together on Jefferies' holdings, so I keep up with what he's doing the way he does with me."

"What's he think about your new partnership?"

"He thinks it's a good investment. He's enthusiastic about it, and why wouldn't he be?"

Emilio was propped on the mound of cushions, one long leg stretched out, one leg bent with his arm resting on his knee while he held his glass of champagne. Turned on his side, he was only inches away from her while he waited for her answer.

She shrugged. "I suppose you're right."

"Do you ever take time off?" Emilio asked her.

"Not often. I will in the future. I don't need to now."

"So my partner is a workaholic," he said, picking up a menu. "I need to show you how to enjoy life," he said, handing her a menu.

She leaned back against the pillows to read the suggestive choices, yet the food described beneath the names sounded savory, and she already knew it was first-rate.

"See anything you like?" he asked in a deep voice.

"Of course. It all looks yummy."

"Yummy's right," he repeated, his eyes steadily on her and she suspected he was not referring to the dinner items listed. "Delectable, enticing and I'm starving." With every word his voice dropped and became more of a rasp.

"Concentrate, Emilio, on food," she rejoined, as always her breathlessness betraying her reaction to him.

Smiling, he returned to reading his menu. She looked at his thick eyelashes and his wavy hair that she could too easily imagine combing through her fingers.

"I hope you've found something tasty for dinner," he said.

"I know what I want," she said, closing her menu.

"And so do I," he said, giving her a long look that made her pulse race again.

Emilio pushed a button and within minutes, a waiter knocked and entered to take their orders. Conscious of Emilio's unwavering regard on her, she ordered a fruit and rum drink with her pork tenderloin. When Emilio ordered their appetizers, Cabernet with an entrée of crusted beef tenderloin, and his attention was on the waiter, she took the opportunity to let her focus drift over his length. This tall, appealing man had altered her business already, simply by becoming her partner. What other changes lay ahead? she wondered. She looked up to find him watching her with a faint smile.

"So what are your ambitions, Brittany? What do you want in your future?"

"Right now, I'm totally focused on making Brittany Beach a success," she replied.

"And once it is—then what?"

"I think that'll be sufficient to keep me busy as long as I want to be involved in it. I don't have to try to own half of South Beach the way my brothers seem aimed to."

"You didn't say a word about romance, a partner outside the business, even marriage or a family. Are you burned out on families?"

"Not at all," she denied, aware of Emilio stretched out beside her. "In the future, I want my own family and children someday, but I'm not in a rush. Right now, Brittany Beach takes my time. It won't always."

"With a partner, that should ease slightly."

"So you'll see to it that I have time to get out with men and fall in love," she teased.

One of his dark eyebrows arched. "You're misreading my intentions in this partnership if you think I'm here to free you up to go out with other men. I want to get to know you better, myself."

Her pulse gave another skip as she laughed. "I opened the door for that remark. You know I was kidding."

"I wasn't," he answered.

She sipped her drink and stared at him over her glass. "We'll get to know each other at work."

"Yes, we will," he agreed. "And I'm looking forward to it immensely. So far, my time has never been spent better."

"You're back to exaggeration. You're too accustomed to trying to charm your companion."

Amusement flared in his eyes. "While you are going to give me the unvarnished truth. We'll be a challenge to each other."

"No, no! No challenges here," she said quickly with a wave of her fingers. "I don't want to become a project."

"Brittany Beach is a project. You and I are on the way to becoming friends."

"I'll drink to that one," she said, raising her glass and he touched his to hers with a faint clink, his fingers brushing hers. "To our lasting friendship," she said.

"And wherever it leads us," he added, gazing into her eyes and making her breath catch.

The waiter knocked and served a basket of thick bread slices along with their appetizer of golden tiger shrimp. He poured small saucers of oil and balsamic vinegar for dipping their bread and then they were alone again.

"So what was growing up like?" she asked him and he shrugged.

"I had a good life. I remember moments with my birth mother, but I was only three when she died. The Jefferies were the parents I knew and they gave me opportunities that I would never have had, otherwise."

"They're not still living, are they?" she asked, vaguely remembering hearing that they had both died.

He shook his head. "No. Jordan and I were backpacking across Europe after graduating from college when our folks died in a boating accident."

"I'm sorry, Emilio. That's dreadful! Do you and Jordan get along?"

"Sure. Since Jordan and I are the same age, we're close and, at the same time, we've had our share of brotherly battles, but it was kid stuff, competition. We're both strong-willed."

"So you admit that," she teased.

He shrugged and tugged a lock of her hair. "I suspect someone else in this room is a strong-willed person."

She smiled. "My family sees me as the baby. Even my twin sister does. That's why I'm so determined to make a go of Brittany Beach," she admitted. "I don't tell most people that, Emilio."

"Good. I hope you share things with me. That's what a friend is for," he said. "I understand about families. I was the adopted son, so I always thought I had to keep up with Jordan."

"I imagine you did," she said.

He shrugged. "Well enough," he answered. Studying her, he placed his fork on his plate. "I've known a lot of women, but I haven't had a lot of females who were important friends. You're easy to talk to and you're a good listener and, as partners, we may have a special relationship."

"I hope we're friends. We're going to have to trust each other."

He looked down and touched his fork. She drank some of

her water and when he looked up, his expression was solemn. "Brittany…" He paused and she waited.

"What is it?" she asked.

"I hope we're best friends," he finished finally and she smiled at him, yet she had the feeling he had been about to say something else and she wondered if something bothered him.

The waiter appeared with their entrées and conversation shifted back to food and the restaurant.

After the first bite of her tender pork, she sighed. "This is delicious! No wonder you have such a crowd. People will always come for food like this."

"I'm glad you like it," he said easily.

She took another bite and closed her eyes to savor it as she chewed. "Emilio, this is absolutely scrumptious."

"I hope I can evoke that kind of reaction in you sometime," he said in a husky voice, and she opened her eyes to find him watching her.

Her appetite fled and awareness of Emilio took its place. She took a deep breath as she reached for her wine and sipped, watching him. She felt consumed by his green gaze that conveyed his desire. She set down her glass and waved her fingers at him. "Go back to you dinner," she whispered.

"There are other things I'd rather do," he said in a voice that had lowered another notch.

"Right now, we're sticking to dinner," she said, hoping she sounded matter-of-fact and more calm than she felt. He sat so close and his expression was so intent that she found it difficult to get back to a more impersonal level.

"These beds cause all kinds of trouble."

"Au contraire!" he said in a soft voice. "This is one of the best dinners I've ever had."

"You go back to concentrating on your beef," she said. "And I'll do the same with mine."

"I'm concentrating," he answered and she looked up at him, knowing he wasn't focusing on his dinner. When she pointed to his plate, he smiled.

Her appetite had diminished and she noticed that his was not great, either, in spite of the delicious cuisine. He had already ordered dessert and they ate a few bites of a decadent chocolate concoction they shared before she put down her fork and sat back.

"Thanks for the fabulous meal," she said.

"We can at least dance off dinner," he suggested.

"I agree with you on that," she replied, standing when he did and slipping into her pumps again.

"Which dance floor—our outdoor pavilion and Latin music, or the main dining room with its dance floor."

"I'll take the pavilion," she replied. They strolled through a small lush garden. A bar stretched along one corner of the pavilion and tables formed a semicircle around the dance floor and bar.

After getting a table and ordering drinks, Emilio held her chair. "Excuse me a moment, Brittany. I need to make a quick call."

She nodded and enjoyed watching the dancers while Emilio was gone. When he returned, he took her hand to lead her to the dance floor where he turned her to face him for a tango. His every move was seductive, a reminder of his fit, muscular body.

As they danced, his hot gaze followed every move she made, leaving her warm and flushed. She was aware they had left business in the dust and the evening had changed from a celebration of work.

After half a dozen dances, they returned to their table. "I can see more reasons why this restaurant is so successful," she said, sipping her bottled water.

It was two in the morning before she realized the time and told him she should go.

"Come by the office. I have something to seal our bargain."

Curious, she slanted him a look, but went along with him as he took her arm.

He turned on one soft light and disappeared into his bar, leaning down to pick up something. When he came out of the bar, he carried a large box wrapped in white paper and tied with a huge red ribbon. He carried it to a credenza and set it down. "A present to remember this day and night and the beginning of a fantastic partnership," he said.

Surprised, she looked up at him. "You shouldn't have done this."

"I wanted to," he said quietly. "Go ahead. Open your present."

She started to pick it up and discovered it was heavy. Surprised, she glanced at Emilio, who stood patiently waiting. She carefully unfastened the large red silk bow. "This is too beautiful to open."

"Presents are for opening and enjoying," he said, looking amused. "I didn't know it would be such a production to get into. Christmas and birthdays must take you hours and hours."

She wrinkled her nose at him. "This bow is far too pretty to demolish. I'm excited, but I don't have a present for you."

"That's not the point here. I'm doing what I want to do," he said. "Of course, I didn't expect a production of opening a gift. I do have a knife."

"Heavens, no! We're not cutting this ribbon," she said and bent over to undo the knot. When she had trouble, he joined her and tugged on a piece of the ribbon, leaning near enough that she could detect his enticing aftershave.

"There," he said, and she pulled the bow free and carefully wound up the ribbon and placed it on the table. She tore open the paper to find a large, plain white box.

"I can't imagine," she said, glancing at him while her curiosity grew.

He shrugged. "There's a way to find out," he said, smiling.

She tugged off the lid and gasped as she looked at the Richardson painting. She whirled to look at the empty place on his wall where the painting had been. "Emilio, you can't give me this!"

"I can and I have," he said, smiling at her while he stood with his hands on his hips. He walked up to her and her pulse drummed. She looked at the painting again.

"When did you box this up?"

"Before we started dancing. Andino wrapped it for me and got one of the women to tie the bow. Rather a nice job of wrapping."

"I can't take your painting."

He laughed. "After battling me tooth and nail for it at the auction? Come on—you love it and you know it."

"Yes, but it's yours and it's valuable."

"It's a gift from me to you, Brittany. I want you to have it in celebration of our partnership. Take it and enjoy it."

She drew a deep breath and turned to look at him again. Impulsively, she threw her arms around his neck to hug him. "Thank you! What a marvelous gift!"

Instantly, his arm banded her waist and he held her tightly. She leaned back to look up at him, framing his face with her hands, feeling the faintest growth of stubble beneath her palms.

The minute her lips touched his, his tongue touched her and her mouth opened to him.

His tongue stroked hers, stirring erotic sensations. He wrapped his other arm tightly around her, holding her against his hard length. Her heart slammed against her ribs and she felt as if she were standing in flames.

She returned his kiss passionately as her tongue stroked his. Her pulse roared in her ears and time vanished. She tightened her arms around his neck and wound her fingers in his hair. Desire ignited and she ached for him, holding him tightly, forgetting everything else except his kisses.

How much time passed, she didn't know. Her heart pounded and Emilio's hand slid up her back and he caressed her nape, heightening her need.

Realizing how passionately she kissed him, she pushed gently against his chest.

Immediately, he raised his head and studied her with a smoldering gaze. Her heart still thudded and she hoped she could catch her breath and find her voice. She leaned inches more away from him.

"I didn't mean for that to happen," she whispered, looking into his green eyes that had darkened to the color of a stormy sea.

"I'm glad it did," he said in return, still holding her, studying her features. She shook her head.

"No. We're business partners. I meant to keep things professional between us," she said with her quiet tone covering her stormy emotions, because his kiss had been sensational. She pushed again lightly and he released her.

"Professional went out the window when we began having a long phone conversation and becoming good friends. Tonight, there's dinner, dancing." His eyes twinkled. "And the evening isn't over yet," he said.

"It's near enough over." Smiling, she shrugged. "You're a sexy man. Just don't take my heart."

"I'm a sexy man," he repeated in a husky voice. "Now that really did make my day."

She glanced at the picture, thinking of a way to change the subject. "I want you to know that I love my gift and I'll treasure it."

"Good. That's what I want you to do," he replied, still watching her. "And wipe out a memory of us fighting over it."

Smiling, she shook her head. Overwhelmed by his kiss that had stirred her more than she would have dreamed possible, she tried to gather her wits. She turned to look at the painting again, running her index finger carefully along a corner of the frame. "This really is beautiful."

He came to stand beside her to look at the painting. She was acutely conscious that his arm grazed hers.

"I don't want to carry something this valuable home tonight when I'm alone."

"Wait and I'll bring it to your house when you want me to."

She looked up at him and her pulse jumped again as she saw the desire that still burned in his eyes. "Tomorrow night, eat dinner at my house. I'll come get the painting and, if you want, you can ride back with me."

"I'll be there for dinner and I'll bring the painting." She told him the combination to get through the gate at her condo.

"Emilio, the gift is wonderful! I'm so thrilled. Thank you," she said again, turning to face him.

He placed a hand on her shoulder. "This doesn't mean that I won't outbid you again at another auction," he said, and she smiled.

"Next time, I may not give up so easily."

"I don't think you gave up easily on this one. Now it's yours, and if it hadn't been for you, I could have had it for much less."

"Don't complain, you got it. Only now it's *mine*," she said, laughing and excited over his gift. She turned to face him again. "What a wonderful evening you've shown me! It's been fabulous."

He crossed the room with her and held open the door. "I'll go out with you."

"Do you have a picture to put in place of the one you gave me?"

"Not now, but I'll get one," he replied casually. "No problem."

When they left the front of the restaurant, he took the stub from her to give to the valet to bring her car. As soon as it arrived, Emilio tipped the valet and went around to open her door himself. As soon as she was seated, he leaned down. "I look forward to tomorrow night and I'll call you in a while," he said.

"Thanks a million. Good night, Emilio."

As he stepped back, she drove away, glancing in the rearview mirror to see him watching her. Her lips still tingled from his kisses.

The evening had been fabulous. She liked his company. His kisses burned her to cinders and dancing with him had ignited desire.

Excitement bubbled in her and she was anxious to get home and talk to him some more. She was shocked to have a partner, to have her debt erased, to have the Richardson oil painting, but, most of all, she was surprised to discover how much she enjoyed Emilio and how much she responded to him. Once again, she reminded herself that was probably the same reaction as most women he knew.

When she entered her empty condo her phone was ringing, and she dropped her purse and made a dash to yank up the receiver and answer.

Smiling when she heard Emilio's voice, she switched on lights and stretched out on her bed to talk. He'd called to say good night and after a quick chat, they broke the connection.

Humming and smiling, she got ready for bed and then was too keyed up to sleep. She kept remembering their fiery kisses that had stirred her more than any others in her life.

Tomorrow night, Emilio would be with her at her place for dinner. She couldn't wait to spend another evening with her new partner. Her fabulous, sexy partner who continued to surprise her.

Five

The next day, Emilio called to say he wouldn't make it by Brittany Beach because he had unexpected situations arise at El Diablo. They arranged to see each other at Brittany's at eight. "You said you like to swim. Bring your suit and we'll swim before dinner," she said.

"Absolutely," he replied. "See you at eight," he added and ended his call.

As the day passed, Brittany wondered how many times she looked at the clock before she finally headed home to get ready for Emilio's visit.

After trying on several outfits, she settled on a blue sundress and sandals. She wore her hair in a thick braid and her anticipation built as she dressed.

Promptly at eight her doorbell chimed.

She opened the door to find Emilio standing with a bottle of wine under his arm, the box in his hands, his swim trunks and towel on top of the box. Dressed in a tan knit shirt and tan slacks, he looked his usual handsome self.

Excited to have him by for dinner, she stepped back and ushered him inside.

His warm gaze slipped over her and she could see the approval in his eyes. "You look great," he said.

"Thanks. Bring the painting in here and, for now, let's put it on the bed in the spare bedroom. Later on, you can help me decide where to hang it."

Emilio followed her into the bedroom to place it on the bed and then he paused to look around at the polished wood floor, wicker furniture and contemporary art on the walls. "Nice room," he said.

"Come on and I'll show you the rest of my place."

She took him through the condo and he looked at everything, stepping into her bedroom to glance at the bed and then at her. "Now I'll be able to picture you in my mind when we talk on the phone and you tell me you're in your bed."

"And that matters?" she asked.

"Sure. I want to know all about you." He crossed the room to place his hands on her shoulders. "I'm discovering I have a fascinating partner."

"I lead an ordinary life," she said.

He grinned. "As if being a Garrison is an 'ordinary life.'"

"Mine isn't so unusual. Hey, it's been a hot, steamy day. Want to swim first?"

"Sure."

"You can change in the other bedroom and meet me at the pool. It's right through the door off my dining room." She left to change into her two-piece dark blue swimsuit and its cover-up. When she approached the pool, he bobbed up, shook his head and swam toward the edge in long, powerful strokes.

Splashing water, he climbed out and her pulse jumped. His

body was lean and muscular. Muscles rippled with every move he made. His taut biceps bulged and he had a mat of dark curls across his chest. He was deeply tanned with his naturally olive skin turned even darker by the hot Florida sunshine. He wore narrow, low-riding trunks and she inhaled deeply. His washboard belly was flat, revealed by the low suit.

She kicked off her flip-flops and dropped her cover-up on a chaise lounge and turned to find him watching her. Desire blazed in his green eyes as they traveled over her.

"You look great! You serve dinner like that and you'll pack 'em into Brittany Beach."

She laughed. "If I serve dinner wearing this, I'll be arrested. Race you across the pool to the far corner," she said, striding past him and jumping in to swim as fast as she could.

She knew when he caught up with her. She had given herself a head start and now she fought to keep up with him, wanting to beat him and wondering why she was so competitive. In seconds, he pulled ahead and when she reached the corner, he was already there with his arms stretched out on the sides of the pool as he lounged and waited for her. "Beat you," he said, teasing her. "You're competitive, Brittany."

"Only sometimes and in certain things. Maybe you bring it out in me," she said and his grin widened.

She splashed water on him and he caught her wrists, playfully trying to dunk her. She grew up with brothers and she twisted to grab his shoulders to take him down with her. They both went under, struggling and then bobbing up and laughing.

He caught her around the waist and yanked her to him. She thought he was going to dunk her again and she reached to hold him, but then she looked into his eyes and her breath caught.

She could tell he wanted her and she knew he was going to kiss her. She became aware of her legs against his, her body pressed against his. He was wet and warm and solid hard

SARA ORWIG 69

muscles. His arm tightened around her waist, drawing her against him.

Her heart pounded as her breasts pressed against his chest. Her lips parted and she looked at his mouth. He lowered his head to brush her lips with his. With a soft moan, she wrapped her arms around his neck and pulled his head down to her. "I said I wasn't going to do this and here I am, doing it again," she whispered.

He covered her mouth with his, his tongue sliding into her mouth to stroke her. She was hot, suddenly burning, even though she was in cold water. She clung to Emilio, kissing him passionately, holding him, aware they were almost naked in each other's arms. She let one hand slide over his smooth, muscled back.

She moved her hips against him as his hand followed the curve of her back, down over her bottom, heightening her desire.

While she kissed Emilio deeply and as passionately as he kissed her, her pulse drowned out all other sounds except the roaring in her ears. She ached for him, wanting more, knowing she was getting more involved with him every time they were together.

She pushed against him and leaned back. "This isn't a private pool," she whispered, barely knowing what she was saying. He looked as if he could devour her. He inhaled deeply and released her, regarding her with a hunger that made her feel as if he wanted her more than anything else on earth. She swam away from him and then turned when she had put yards between them.

"We've had our swim. I'll dress and get us drinks," she said while they both treaded water. She wondered if he knew how badly she wanted to keep on kissing him.

He nodded and disappeared underwater. She swam to the edge and climbed out, retrieving her cover-up and glancing back to find him at the side of the pool watching her.

Warming beneath his steady gaze, she pulled on the blue cover-up, slipped into her flip-flops and headed for the gate. Her back prickled and she knew his eyes followed her every move.

She hurried inside and showered, pulling her hair free and drying it. Thinking about him, she dressed again in her sundress and sandals and tied her hair behind her head with a blue ribbon. His kisses had increased her desire and she knew her awareness of him would be even more intense.

She found him in the kitchen with two glasses of wine.

"I hope you don't mind," he began, but when he turned to look at her, he stopped. "Look at you."

He crossed the room to her and her pulse jumped, as it did constantly when he was near. "Your hair is down," he said, reaching behind her head to tug the blue ribbon free. "I like you this way," he said with a hoarse note in his deep voice.

She shook her head slightly and smiled at him. "It's just plain hair," she said.

"You look great," he said softly.

"Thanks. And you started to say something about me not minding—not minding what?" she asked.

He put her ribbon on a table and turned. "I hope you don't care that I got our drinks. I rummaged around and found glasses. I started the grill on your patio because I saw the steaks you have marinating in the fridge. Unless those are for another night," he said, picking up the glasses of wine and crossing the room to hand her a drink.

"They're for tonight and, my, aren't you efficient to have around."

"You'd be surprised what I can do," he said with a faint smile.

She tilted her head to study him. "Now that does make me wonder. In the meantime, I'll add efficient to your good qualities."

"You say that like there's a list of good qualities and a list of bad. Is there?"

"Do you have a guilty conscience?" she teased.

"No, I don't," he said, smiling at her, but something flickered in his eyes, startling her and she wondered what he was thinking.

"No bad qualities yet that I've discovered," she said. "But I'll qualify it with a 'yet.'"

When he handed her the drink, their fingers brushed and even that slight contact stirred more tingles. "I remember the looks you gave me when we were in the bidding war."

"It's cooler to sit in here," she said, waving her hand toward the room adjoining the kitchen. It was a casual living area with bamboo furniture and had a glass wall that gave a view of the beach and ocean. He followed her down two steps into the room and when she sat on the leather sofa, he sat at the other end, turning to face her.

"Here's to getting to know you better," he said, lifting his glass and extending it to her so she could touch it with hers.

"And to getting to know you, too, Emilio," she replied, thinking about their moment in each other's arms in the pool. "I'd say we're off to a great beginning."

He stretched out a long arm to touch a lock of her hair. She felt a faint tug against her scalp and was aware of his constant scrutiny.

"How many women are in your life? From the media, it looks as if there are too many to count," she asked, her way of reminding him she knew of his magnetism toward women.

"There isn't even one in particular right now. Sounds as if your opinion of me is all wrong where females are concerned."

"I know all the pictures I see."

"Tabloids. You should know better than to put stock in them. So has there ever been a particular man in your life?"

She shrugged. "Not really. The most important was a relationship in college. Long forgotten now."

Emilio smiled. "Good news all around."

"Ready for me to put on the steaks?" she asked, and when he nodded, she stood. Since that first night at Brittany Beach, she had always been conscious of him as a sexy, appealing male, but now, because of their kisses, she was far more aware of the slightest contact with him or even merely when he stood beside her. Occasionally, when he was busy with something, she studied his handsome features and couldn't keep from pausing when she looked at his mouth and remembered his kisses.

Within minutes, he took over the grilling task and she got salads, glasses of water, hot baked potatoes and rolls on the table.

As they ate, she listened to him talk about getting El Diablo started and they compared notes on the beginnings of their two restaurants. After dinner, he helped her clean and put away dishes and the time flew. When they finished, she faced him.

"Now, come with me and help me decide where to hang the painting."

They went to her living room, which had white walls, a polished hardwood floor, bookshelves on one wall. Her furniture was mahogany, more formal, but still with glass tables and contemporary art on the wall. Emilio strolled over to study her Jasper Johns painting.

"Nice, Brittany," Emilio said. He turned to look at the walls.

"I think I want the picture above my sofa," she said, waving her hand toward the plain deep blue sofa. "What do you think?"

"I think what you want is what's best. You're the one who lives here," he said. He walked over to place the Richardson painting carefully on a table and then he returned to lift down the picture that already hung over the sofa. He stood it on the floor and propped it against a wall.

Brittany watched him work, seeing the muscles flex in his back as his knit shirt clung to him. She thought about the moments in the pool when they had been locked in each other's arms and all but naked with only tiny strips of cloth between them. Desire made her hot and her gaze ran over him.

He turned and she looked up to meet his curious gaze. She could feel her cheeks grow warm.

"Can you hold the picture there?" she asked, hating the breathlessness in her voice.

"Sure," he said, pulling the sofa out from the wall slightly. He picked up the picture and held it out, centered behind the sofa.

"I think that looks wonderful. Emilio, I'll tell you again, you shouldn't have given it to me, but I love it!"

"That's what I hoped. After all, you fought tooth and nail for it," he said. "Actually, maybe it'll hang right where the one I took down was. Let's see how it looks."

After he hung it in place, he stepped back and pushed the sofa where it had sat. "What do you think?" he asked her.

"I think the painting looks perfect there. It's where it belongs."

"So do I get another hug and kiss?" he asked.

"Maybe later," she said, smiling at him. "Now I want the painting you removed to go somewhere else." She looked around. "Do you mind holding it over there for me?" She pointed to a space on another wall and he held the picture for a few moments before she shook her head. She asked him to try it elsewhere until she found the spot she liked.

"I'll hang it for you if you have the equipment."

"I can get the carpenter who does work here," she said. "Shall we sit in here to talk where I can look at my painting?" She motioned to a chair. She sat in a wingback chair and he sat in another near her. "This is far more exciting to have the painting now than it would have been if I'd outbid you. I really appreciate owning it."

"So I'm forgiven for outbidding you?"

"I didn't say that," she teased. "No, you're not, and I suspect if we end up at another auction, you'll do exactly the same thing if we both want something again."

"I'm not admitting to that when it might not ever happen," he said, stretching out his long legs and crossing them at his ankles. "So if you ever take time off, what do you like to do besides swim?"

"I like to go to flea markets and art galleries."

"So far, we share the same likes. Do you hike?"

"I never have. Where do you hike around here?"

"You don't around here. Okay, sometime soon, take some time and you show me your favorite galleries and I'll show you mine," he said.

"Deal. I have a couple of new artists I'm watching," she said, studying the picture across the room. She was still surprised he had given it to her and she was so thrilled to have it that she found it difficult to keep from looking at it constantly.

"This erases all the bad thoughts I had about you after the auction," she said, smiling at him.

"I figured you had some dark thoughts about me after you left that day." He grinned. "So now I'm in your good graces. Getting it and then giving it back to you both have definitely been worth my while," he said, his voice dropping a notch.

She knew he was talking about her kiss last night. "I'll enjoy my painting and you tell me about hiking," she said, to get back on a less volatile subject. She listened while Emilio talked about a hiking trip and they went from one topic to another. Later, they went to the kitchen to get pop for her and a cold beer for him before they sat at the kitchen table and talked more.

Finally, with a glance at his watch, Emilio stood. "It's time. Actually, way past time, since it's two in the morning."

She walked to the door with him, where he turned to her. "The steaks were great. The company was even better."

Looking into his green eyes, she saw the desire that she felt. "Thanks again for the picture. What a fabulous gift!"

When his gaze lowered to her mouth, her pulse raced. "This has been a great evening," he said and slipped his arm around her waist, drawing her to him. She placed her hands on his arms, feeling the solid muscles while she looked up at him and wondered if he could hear the pounding of her heart.

"Emilio," she whispered.

Leaning slightly, he covered her mouth with his. When his tongue went into her mouth, he tightened his arm, pulling her up against him as he leaned over her.

With her heart racing, Brittany wound her arm around his neck and clung to him as she kissed him in return. Thrusting her hips against him, she felt his arousal hard against her.

He leaned farther, turning slightly while he slipped his hand along her back and over her bottom. As he pulled her up tightly against him, she moaned. Desire rocked her and she clung to him to keep from reaching for his buttons.

He slipped his hand to her throat and then down to follow the straight neckline of her sundress. His hand drifted feather-light over her dress, down over her breast and a tremor shook her. She tightened her arms around his neck and shifted her hips tighter against him.

While he kissed her passionately, he wrapped both arms around her waist. Finally, she pushed against his shoulders and he released her. She opened her eyes to find him watching her with a smoldering gaze and such desire that she wanted to step right back into his arms. But she knew she shouldn't.

"We have to stop now," she said, trying to get her breath.

"It's been a great night," he said. "Will I see you tomorrow?"

She shook her head. "I doubt it. I take off during the day

and then late in the afternoon I go to Bal Harbour for our family dinner."

"Afterward?"

"I usually go home, unless there's a problem."

"You may have a weather problem tomorrow. The hurricane is heading this way, but it's losing force. They still expect a terrific storm that should hit about midnight tomorrow night or in the early hours of the morning." He hesitated for a moment. "It's been a great evening, Brittany."

"I think so, too," she said while he played with a lock of her hair. After a moment he gave a gentle tug on her hair and let go.

"Take care and thanks again for dinner. I'm glad to see where you live."

"I imagine you'll be back," she said lightly.

"I hope so," he replied and brushed a feathery kiss on her mouth before he turned to go out the door. She stepped outside and watched his long stride as he went to his car, climbed in and drove out of sight.

She shut and locked her door and returned to the living room to look at her new painting, but her thoughts were on their kisses in the pool this afternoon. She still tingled from the kisses they'd just had.

In a short time, she wasn't surprised to hear her phone ring and she rushed to answer it in her bedroom, where she could stretch out in bed and talk.

"What were you doing?" Emilio asked when she said hello. "Let me guess the answer to my own question. You were still looking at your painting."

Smiling, she lay on her pillows and propped one foot on her other knee. "You guessed exactly right. How intuitive of you."

"Do you like it for the painting itself or because you got it after all?"

"How can you ask that! Because of the painting," she insisted, laughing at his question. "It's fabulous and I think you're fantastic for giving it to me."

"Next time we're together, you show me exactly how fantastic you think I am."

"Instead, sometime I'll cook you another steak dinner," she replied.

"That's not the same at all. So what are you doing right now and how are you dressed or undressed?"

She smiled and answered him, going on to other topics until she looked at the clock and saw they had talked over an hour. "Emilio, I have to go or I won't be able to get up in the morning."

"It was a great evening," he told her again and said goodbye and broke the connection.

She got ready for bed and then returned to her living room to sit for another ten minutes to look at the painting, finally crawling into bed to dream about Emilio.

She slept late and as she ate breakfast, Emilio called to talk again, finally telling her goodbye.

She did chores around her place that she needed to do and talked to him once again about three that afternoon until she had to get off the phone to dress for her family dinner.

Brittany wore pale yellow slacks and a yellow silk shirt. She wished she had an excuse to miss this dinner—often the siblings weren't all there—but she thought she'd draw less attention if she attended it.

She tried to calm her nerves, hoping her hawkeyed brothers paid little attention to her, particularly her ambition-driven oldest brother, Parker. Hopefully, by nine o'clock she could escape and the ordeal would be over.

In ritzy Bal Harbour, she swept through the wide stone pillars to the estate and stopped next to Parker's convertible.

Inside, as she hurried across the silent foyer with its sweeping staircase and thick stone pillars, she encountered Lisette Wilson, their longtime housekeeper.

"Ah, Miss Brittany, I'm glad you're here," Lisette said, a faint smile crossing her features as she patted Brittany's wrist.

"How could I miss Sunday dinner?" Brittany responded brightly. "Where's the family?"

"On the veranda wondering when the storm will hit. Dinner will be announced in minutes."

"Then I better join them. I'm late and Mother's going to be unhappy with me."

"These days, she's unhappy with the whole world," Lisette said, her eyes clouding with worry and a frown creasing her wrinkled brow.

"Sorry, Lisette. I know you take good care of her. I don't know what we'd do without you."

"I've been with her a long time—with all of you, for that matter," she said, turning away.

Brittany squared her shoulders, already knowing that her mother's drinking had grown worse since her father's death and suspecting that would be confirmed again in seconds.

She found her family standing on the veranda with its view of the pool and, beyond the pool, the blue ocean. In the far distance, storm clouds were rolling in and Brittany knew bad weather was forecast for later that night.

The moment she stepped onto the veranda, Brooke and Brittany exchanged a look. For a second, Brittany had an instinctive feeling something was bothering Brooke and then the moment was gone as Brooke gave Brittany a vague smile.

Brooke stood talking to Parker, Anna Cross, Parker's fiancée, and Stephen. All greeted Brittany as she approached them. She paused where her mother was seated, smiling at Bonita, who clutched an almost-empty glass in her hand.

"You're really late," Bonita complained, the frown wrinkles in her brow deepening.

"There was a traffic tie-up on Collins that delayed me," Brittany answered truthfully.

"I'd think you'd put the family first when it's only once a week, but without your father, you probably don't want to come home," Bonita said sharply, her words thick and slightly slurred. Dark circles beneath Bonita's eyes had developed since the reading of the will, and Brittany knew her mother did nothing to hide her bitterness over the discovery of another child by their father. Even so, it was difficult to conjure up a lot of sympathy, because Bonita was a cold woman.

"I'm here," Brittany reminded her gently, ignoring Bonita's gibe. When she glanced at Brooke, she saw her twin bite her lip. Bonita's sharp words, even when directed at Brittany, could disturb Brooke.

"Hi, Brooke," Brittany greeted her sister, turning from Bonita, who was finishing her drink. Brittany turned to greet Parker, who had Anna at his side.

"Hi, Brittany," Parker greeted her while Anna smiled.

"Hi, Parker. Anna, it's nice to have you with us," she said. "You're the best thing that has ever happened to my brother."

"I'll agree with that," Parker said, looking fondly at Anna.

"I'm glad," Anna replied. "He's the best thing in my life."

Brittany bit back a sarcastic remark, knowing the two were in love and she didn't want to be unkind to Anna.

"It is getting stormy looking," Brittany said, glancing beyond them at the bank of dark clouds.

"We're in for a tropical storm tonight," Parker said, also looking at the ocean. "They downgraded the hurricane, but we'll still get wind and rain. I hope we're out of here before it hits. It's difficult enough on a sunny day to fight the traffic from here to SoBe."

"I'll leave early," Brittany said, seeing a chance to escape sooner than she had thought. "I want to make sure everything is all right at the restaurant."

"Good idea," Parker agreed. "We should all leave earlier tonight," he added, looking at Anna as if his reason for leaving early had nothing to do with a storm. The warmth in Parker's gaze always surprised Brittany. Her calculating brother was actually in love and it showed. Never would she have guessed that even Parker would be love struck, but since Anna had come into his life, he was in a daze most of the time when Brittany saw him.

"Hi, Brit. I saw the celebrity you had in your club Friday night," Stephen said, joining them. Bonita called to him and he left the group.

"I saw the picture, too," Parker said. "My congratulations. Seems Brittany Beach is drawing an illustrious crowd."

"Thanks, that gives me a warm, fuzzy feeling, Big Brother."

"Do I take that at face value or is there a little bite in it?" Parker asked in a noncommittal voice.

"I meant it. You're all Mr. Bottom Line, even more than Dad was. I'm happy when you're pleased with Brittany Beach. And speaking of Garrison holdings," she said, hoping to get off the topic of her restaurant, "are there any developments about our newly discovered sibling?"

Parker frowned and swirled a drink he had barely touched. "No. She's not interested in us, it seems."

"What a bomb Dad dropped on us," Adam remarked in what was almost a whisper as he joined them and greeted Brittany. "Mother seems to be having a worse time dealing with this, as time goes by, instead of the other way around. Sorry, Anna, but you're part of the family now and all that goes with sharing our lives."

Bonita was across the veranda, chatting with Stephen, both

talking in low voices. Brittany watched them a moment, marveling once again that Stephen was the one sibling who was never the target of their mother's biting criticisms. With the increase in their mother's drinking, Brittany wondered if that would change.

Her mind wandered from the conversation. She relaxed a degree because, so far, no one in the family seemed to have heard about the embezzlement or her new partner. If any of her siblings had, he—or she—would have already said something, Brittany was certain. She fought the temptation to glance at her watch. She knew she had only been there minutes, but she willed the time to pass.

It seemed aeons before dinner was announced, and she noticed that Stephen helped Bonita, who was unsteady on her feet. Brittany could see the grim tightening of Stephen's jaw and knew his disapproval of their mother's drinking was increasing at the same time that Bonita's overindulgence was growing.

The family entered the elegant dining room with its illuminated oil paintings, the ornate ceiling and a low-hanging chandelier. Again, Brittany was amused and surprised to see Parker hovering over Anna as he led her into the dining room.

While talk was lively around the table, Brittany's mind constantly wandered, back to Emilio, to her fear of discovery of her new partner before she was ready.

She glanced around the table, thinking about all their businesses from their father and how each sibling fought for success: Parker, CEO of Garrison, Inc., always kept an eye on everybody's business and usually managed at Sunday dinner to inquire about each sibling's current situation. Stephen owned Garrison Grand, a SoBe premier luxury hotel. Adam, younger than Stephen and Parker, had made a success of Estate, his popular nightclub. Brooke, who was unusually quiet, had The Sands, a luxury condominium building.

Remarks were made about each business, but when Brittany said her week had gone well, Adam mentioned a singer who had been photographed at Brittany Beach and later at Estate and the conversation shifted from Brittany's restaurant to his club.

Finally, to her relief, dinner was over and they adjourned to the veranda once more. With storm clouds approaching, the sky had darkened to indigo. When Parker got the weather report from CNN, they all listened.

"The storm's moving in earlier than predicted and we're going to get high winds and rain within the hour," Parker said, repeating what had been announced. "If any of you need my help, Anna and I can follow you back," he offered to Brittany, who shook her head quickly.

"Thanks, Parker, I'll be fine and I have generators," she said. "But I'll head there now. I'd like to get to the restaurant before the storm hits." She gave Bonita a perfunctory kiss on the cheek and realized her mother was a zombie and totally out of their conversation.

As quickly as possible, Brittany left to fight her way through traffic to SoBe.

She was halfway when the wind whipped up and in minutes, big drops of rain pelted her car. She turned into a parking lot and got out her cell to call the restaurant, telling Hector to get generators if the electricity went off and to put their portable red neon Open sign out near the curb.

"I'll be right there as soon as possible," she promised before she broke the connection and returned her attention to the highway, all worries about family replaced by concern for Brittany Beach.

Six

As she drove, the storm intensified. Wind bent palm trees and set signs flapping. Brittany's anxicty increased when rain began to fall in sheets, making driving slower and more difficult.

Electricity was out in SoBe and when she finally turned onto Brittany Beach's drive, she was thankful to see its neon lights shimmering through the rain and the red neon Open sign blazing brightly at the curb.

Inside, one of the first employees she saw was Hector, who rushed up to her. "Our generators are running," he said. "Business is booming because the rain has driven people off the street and the beach." She thought how they closed Washington Avenue to cars at night and the street filled with people, musicians, vendors, tourists, a mob that would all have to get somewhere inside tonight.

"We've got a huge crowd," Hector continued. "The lobby is packed and customers may have to wait two hours for a table."

"Serve them complimentary mojitos," she instructed. "The drinks should make the wait more tolerable. If they don't want a mojito, offer a soft drink. Pass something to them to nibble on. Get some kind of simple hors d'oeuvres that will be easy to replenish."

"I'll tell the kitchen right away," he said and left.

"Brittany…"

Instantly her pulse jumped because she recognized Emilio's deep voice. She turned to face him. In navy slacks and a navy cotton shirt, he stopped to comb his fingers through his wet hair.

As he walked up to her, his eyes swept over her with warm approval. "I thought I'd see if you need help, but looks as if you're doing fine," he said.

"We have generators," she said.

"Very good," he said, sounding relieved. "There are places that don't have backup power, and they're out of business until the electricity is restored, which may take a while because I've heard there are large residential areas without power."

"What are you doing out in this?"

"I wanted to see if you needed help," he said, glancing past her. "It doesn't look as if you do, and Brittany Beach appears to be busier than ever."

"Apparently, it is," she replied, self-conscious that her hair was windblown and her clothes damp. "Actually, I just got here, myself. Want to come with me to look around and see what's going on?"

"Sure. Maybe there's something I can do to help."

As they entered the main dining room that was packed with people, she glanced through the wide arch and glimpsed the crowd waiting to get a table. "We're serving complimentary mojitos and hors d'oeuvres to people in the lobby while they wait," she told Emilio and received another nod of approval.

"Good. When I came, people were still arriving."

The minute she stepped into the kitchen, she knew something was awry because people were scurrying around and voices were raised and her executive chef's hat was askew, his straight black hair sticking out in all directions. Angier saw her and rushed to her, waving his thin hands.

"We're running out of food. There's a record crowd, and we can't get dinners cooked quickly enough. Orders are backing up."

"Tell me what you need," she said. "We'll get it from somewhere. Let's get some grills out. Put them on the covered part of the veranda and grill outside."

"Two cooks can't get here and, with such a crowd, we're shorthanded," he complained.

"I'll see about the food," Brittany said.

"I'll do what I can to help in here," Emilio offered as she took the list of needed items and left to hurry to her office. She was already on her cell phone, starting her search. For the next half hour she forgot Emilio as she made calls and found places that could rush the supplies they needed.

When she returned to the kitchen an hour later, order had been restored. Rain still drummed steadily and she walked outside onto the covered area of the veranda to see about the grilling. Surprised, she found Emilio in an apron. His dark hair was tangled on his forehead as he turned skewers with shrimp and pork.

She hurried over to him. "You're cooking? I can do that instead of you," she offered.

"You keep up with everything else," Emilio said. "I can grill. If I go out to see about customers, some reporter will pick up on it. We don't want that happening this early."

Nodding, she returned to the dining room. To her amazement, people waiting to be seated still lined the lobby. The complimentary drinks were flowing and as she moved through the crowd and into the dining room, she was relieved to find that everyone she talked to seemed to be having a good time.

The dining room crowd was equally festive. Occasionally, she would find someone who needed to pay their bill or get a drink and she hurried to meet the needs of her customers.

She lost track of time until she realized the lobby was empty and the place had quieted. She left the bar area to go to the veranda, where the grills were off and no one was outside. When she entered the kitchen, Emilio still cooked. He had shed his shirt and wore a white undershirt with an apron over it. His brown body glistened with sweat. In spite of the air-conditioning, exhausts and fans, with all the cooking and the rain and damp, steamy air outside, the kitchen was hot. His muscles rippled as he picked up containers and moved around the kitchen and, for an instant, she forgot everything else, mesmerized by the sight of his muscular back. His shoulders were broad and his biceps bulged and, again, she recalled that moment locked in his arms in the pool. Dark waves of hair fell over his forehead and her mouth went dry while desire sent her temperature soaring.

She realized how she was staring and, with an effort, she tried to get her mind on business. Crossing the kitchen to him, she took a knife from his hand and placed it on the counter. "I think you can be relieved now," she said. "It's getting quieter out there."

"If you're sure I'm not needed here," he said, stepping to a sink to rinse and dry his hands. He removed the apron and picked up his shirt to pull it on while she watched. He caught her looking at him and paused. Realizing how she had been staring at his chest, he sent her a heated look that fueled her longing.

"I'm ready to call it a night. I've talked to Hector and he's staying and Angier is staying. I'm going home. If you want to follow me, you can come in for a drink."

"That's the best offer I've had in a long time," he said.

"Better than acquiring half of Brittany Beach?" she couldn't resist asking.

He smiled. "Let's go before something happens to put you back to work," he suggested. "Ride with me and I'll bring you tomorrow morning. My place is north of yours."

She nodded, happy to turn the driving over to him.

They had his car brought to the door and drove through rain-drenched streets to her condo. Hand in hand and laughing, they dashed inside. "I'm glad to be here," she exclaimed, kicking off her shoes. "What would you like? I'm having pop. I have wine, beer, pop, water—what'll it be?"

"Beer," he replied, moving around and helping her. They sat at the kitchen table and as she sipped her pop, she glanced at her watch.

"Did you know it's almost four in the morning?"

"Time flew past, but we did all right together, you and I."

"I hope you didn't neglect El Diablo to help at our place," she said, while Emilio reached out to pull the end of the yellow scarf tying back her hair.

Smiling, she shook her head and her thick, brown hair swirled across her shoulders.

Emilio picked up his cold beer. "Here's to my coolheaded partner, who handled the crisis well," he said, raising his bottle in tribute to her. "I'm impressed. You did a great job tonight."

His praise warmed her, and she smiled at him as she raised her pop. "Thank you. I'm glad you think so. With generators and your help, we went smoothly through the storm and about half an hour ago, power was restored."

"Serving complimentary mojitos was perfect. The people in the lobby had their own party. So was putting a neon Open sign out on the curb. That's smart. Getting the needed supplies in the storm was a miracle."

Feeling pleased with his compliments, she smiled. "After the mojitos had been flowing awhile I heard the crowd in front singing together."

"SoBe is a party place. The storm excites people and the atmosphere builds. Suddenly, we have a booming night."

"Booming is right! I hope it calms down tomorrow, although the business was unbelievable. Thanks for your help."

"Glad to," he replied. "I have a great partner."

"Thanks. You sound surprised," she said, wondering what he really thought about her. "We're off to an awesome start." She found some of her fears over rushing into accepting his proposal allayed by his cooperation and diligence through the night.

He leaned forward to take her drink from her hand. "This partnership is far better than I imagined it would be, and I had high expectations," he said in a throaty voice. His eyes darkened and held hers while he slipped his hand behind her head to pull her closer. Leaning forward, he brushed her lips with his.

She drew a deep breath. She was on fire with wanting him. His warm lips brushed hers again, taunting and inviting. She shut her eyes, leaning toward him and then his lips covered hers fully, his tongue going into her mouth and setting her ablaze.

Placing her hand against his chest, she trailed her fingers slowly across his hard muscles and up over his broad shoulder. As he kissed her, she moaned.

She barely noticed when he wrapped his arm around her waist. He pulled her to her feet against him, bending over her to kiss her passionately.

While desire raged, she thrust her hips against him. Leaning away abruptly, he sat on a chair and pulled her onto his lap. His green eyes devoured her, making her feel as if she were the most desirable woman on earth.

"You're beautiful," he said. His voice a rasp as he wound

his fingers in her hair and tilted her head back to kiss her throat. His tongue drew a fiery path from her ear, across her slender throat while her heart thudded. Hot and hard, his thick erection pressed against her hip.

"Emilio," she whispered, scalding sensations bombarding her.

Twisting free the buttons of her silk blouse, he pushed the soft yellow material off her shoulders. Cool air washed over her while he unfastened the clasp of her bra and it fell away. When his big hand cupped her breast, she cried out with pleasure that heightened swiftly. His thumb lazily circled her nipple.

"Emilio, we're going too fast!" she gasped.

"Shh. I know what you want," he whispered and leaned down to take her breast in his mouth. His tongue circled where his thumb had been and she moaned. Wanting all of him, she ached with need. Desperate to kiss him, she wound her fingers in his hair and raised his head.

For one brief moment they looked into each other's eyes. The mirrored desire in depths of green fanned the flames tormenting her. Then she kissed him hungrily, as if it were their first kiss and she had waited a lifetime.

No man had ever kissed her or affected her the way Emilio did effortlessly. A look, a touch could set her pulse pounding and snatch her breath away.

How long they kissed, she didn't know. She felt his hand at her waist and then her slacks were pushed down and his fingers drifted across her bare middle and slipped lower.

Closing her fingers around his wrist, she tugged his hand and stopped him from exploring lower. With an effort she opened her eyes. "Emilio," she whispered.

He raised his head and gave her another burning look that clearly conveyed his desire. "I want to set you on fire," he murmured as he cupped her breasts and watched her while his thumbs circled her nipples.

"You already have," she whispered. Closing her eyes, she moaned and held his wrists. Pleasure enveloped her and desire pushed her toward tossing aside all reservations.

"You want me and you want my kisses," he whispered, leaning down to take a nipple in his mouth and slowly circle the pouting bud with his wet tongue.

She cried out and framed his face in her hands to pull him up to kiss him hotly.

"You melt me and make me want you," she gasped finally as she leaned away. The minute she pushed lightly against his chest, he released her. When he did, she stood, trying to get herself composed and desire under control as she pulled on her clothing. "You're going too fast for me," she said breathlessly.

With a smoldering look as he watched her dress, he came to his feet. "I want you, Brittany."

Fighting the urge to walk back into his arms, she inhaled. "We have to go slow. I can't do this," she said and he nodded, placing his hand against her cheek while he looked at her intently.

"I'll go now," he said, heading for the front. She followed, getting her clothes together. At the door he turned to look at her and scalding desire still burned in his expression and made her pulse skip.

"I'll see you tomorrow," she said.

"I'll pick you up in the morning. Is nine too early?"

"Not at all," she replied.

He glanced at his watch. "That's not so far away. Okay, nine it is. See you in the morning," he said and turned to walk to his car.

She watched his long-legged stride and remembered being in his arms.

Thinking about his hot kisses made her pulse race. Was she

going to be another broken heart in his path? If so, would it jeopardize their business relationship?

Unable to answer her own questions, she locked up and switched off the foyer lights. She thought of Emilio's compliments again and felt another warm rush of pleasure. She knew she was starved for such approval because all her life she had been put down by her family. When it came to praise, she knew her vulnerability. Though she was mindful of how susceptible she might be, Emilio's remarks filled her with satisfaction.

And tonight had laid to rest some of her fears. When Emilio had wanted this partnership, she had jumped at the chance without hesitation or checking to see if there was any reason that it wouldn't be in her interests to accept. Yet tonight he had worked diligently, doing a hot, taxing job that he didn't have to do at all.

Twenty minutes later, her phone rang. Smiling, she picked up the receiver and heard his deep voice.

"Is it too late for a short call?"

"No. After such a hectic night, I'm not that sleepy. Maybe I'll relax while we talk."

"You can doze off and I won't mind. Again, you saved the place with your practical management tonight. I'm getting happier all the time about this partnership."

"Good. So am I," she said, although she thought it was for different reasons than what he was saying. She curled up on her bed to talk to him, listening to his deep voice and the rain still drumming on the windows.

After twenty minutes, she told him good-night and in seconds, she was asleep.

Friday morning, Emilio called to say he would leave his place in about ten minutes and come to Brittany Beach. She replaced the receiver, going to look at herself in her bathroom mirror and comb her hair again.

In a lime-green skirt, sandals and a lime cami with lace across the top and spaghetti straps, she knew he would like her outfit. Her hair was one long braid down her back. She started to comb it out and redo it, but then gave a shake of her head and decided to leave it.

Satisfied with her image, she went to her desk to check over the week's receipts. From the time of the deposit, she had looked often at the books. She could never get enough reassurance that the debt was covered. She'd realized she had exchanged one problem for another. She no longer had to worry about embezzlement, losing Brittany Beach or humiliation with her family. Instead, she fretted about falling in love with Emilio, who was a heartbreaker.

Charming, virile and sexy—she was drawn to him more each hour they spent together.

If he sat in her office even silently poring over books, her concentration was ruined.

She glanced at her watch and decided to check on the kitchen and see if the restaurant had received their supplies for the day. As she crossed the dining room and glanced outside, she saw Parker slow in front and a valet hurry to meet him.

She whirled around and dashed back to her office, yanking out her cell phone to call Emilio. The instant he answered, she cut him off.

"Emilio, come later this morning. Let me call you. Parker is here and I'd just as soon you two don't meet today. Let's give it a bit longer."

"Fine. Call and tell me when you want me to come."

"I will," she said, relief surging and then dying swiftly. Parker never came to Brittany Beach early in the morning. Had he learned about her new partner? When she hurried toward the lobby, she bit her lip. Worry tormented her because she could imagine Parker's ire over her acquiring a partner, even if it was an experienced, successful one.

Looking very much the businessman in his conservative white shirt, navy tie and navy slacks, Parker strode into her lobby. She had to admit, Parker wore authority with as much ease as he wore a tie. A stranger seeing them for the first time would guess Parker was the owner of Brittany Beach, not Brittany. Emilio had that same take-charge air and she wondered as time went by if she would have as difficult a time holding her own with him as she sometimes did with Parker.

"Morning, Brittany."

"And to what do I owe the honor of a visit from you at this hour?" she asked, hoping her voice sounded cheerful and hid her anxiety.

He shrugged. "I had an appointment with a contractor in SoBe. I was in the vicinity and I haven't had breakfast, so I thought I'd stop and catch a bite here if your kitchen is open."

"Sure, come in," she said, relieved to discover his harmless purpose. "I'll join you for coffee. We can eat outside on the veranda or in a cabana tent. It's beautiful this morning," she said, wanting to keep Parker away from the kitchen and her staff, where he could hear about Emilio.

They sat in one of the cabana tents and gazed at blue ocean and blue sky with gulls circling high overhead, occasionally swooping to the water and soaring again. Parker ordered and soon had orange juice, steaming coffee and ham and eggs in front of him.

"I should've called," he said as he ate. "How did you manage through the storm?"

Brittany lowered her coffee cup. "We got along fine. We have generators, so we kept right on serving and cooking. There was a huge crowd. We served complimentary mojitos to the customers waiting for a table—and some had to wait until after two in the morning."

"Good thinking, Brittany, with those drinks," Parker said, studying her while he finished his orange juice.

"Don't sound so grudging, brother dear," she replied, unable to keep the sarcasm out of her voice.

"I meant it. Some places had to close in the storm and some were so bogged down trying to wait on people, that customers left in a huff. Probably a lot came here. Complimentary mojitos was a smart move. I'm sincere in what I said."

"Okay, Parker, truce," she said, knowing it wouldn't last. "I like Anna."

"That's good, because she's part of our family now. How're profits besides the night of the storm?" he asked, going back to the subject of Brittany Beach.

"Still increasing. You'll get the monthly report."

"Good. We're all growing steadily and I'm looking at some more property."

"Our father trained you well. You've filled his shoes as he expected you to do."

"Thanks, but I don't think I can ever do what he did."

"Of course, you can," she said. "Heavens, I didn't think I'd ever hear you cast a shred of doubt on anything you do."

He gave her a crooked smile. "I thought we had a truce, my wicked little sis," he said, and she smiled sweetly at him.

"We do. Want anything else? More toast?"

"Nope. I hate to eat and run," he said, glancing at his watch, "but I've got an appointment back at the office and traffic will already be snarling up."

She strolled to the lobby area with him and stepped outside. "Come back, Parker."

"Sure. Thanks for breakfast. The food was great."

She watched him stride to his car and as soon as his vehicle disappeared, she phoned Emilio, who said he would be at Brittany Beach shortly.

Brittany went back to the receipts and concentrated on work, trying to ignore the image of sea-green, thickly lashed bedroom eyes that danced in her thoughts any time she was apart from Emilio.

Half an hour later she heard a light knock at her office door and when she called to come in, she looked into the warm eyes she had fantasized about through the past hours.

"Good morning," Emilio said in his deep voice as he entered her office. Dressed in a navy knit shirt and gray slacks, he looked refreshed, too handsome.

"Hi," she replied, smiling at him while her heart hammered.

"Think I could talk you into taking a break and having a cup of coffee with me?"

"Yes, you can," she said, tossing aside her pen, knowing her work suffered from his presence. She stood and when his gaze traced over her, one of his dark eyebrows arched and a corner of his mouth lifted in a crooked smile.

"My day has improved vastly," he said in a deeper voice, taking another slower, more thorough assessment that started heat rising until she wanted to fan herself. "The SoBe crowd should flock to Brittany Beach today. At least the males."

"SoBe's filled with women in tight, cool clothes. It's too hot here to be bundled to your chin."

"Thank heavens for that one! And SoBe's not overflowing with women who look like you do. You look great, as usual," he said.

"You'll spoil me with your compliments. Except I remind myself you probably do that with everyone—or maybe every female."

"Hardly. And definitely not everyone," he said, smiling at her while she pressed her intercom to the kitchen to ask for coffee, rolls and orange juice. "It's a pretty morning. Want to sit outside?" she asked, and he nodded.

In minutes, they sat on her private part of the veranda and sipped from steaming cups of black coffee.

"Parker stopped by to eat breakfast because he was in the neighborhood. I think next month we can announce this partnership."

"Don't rush it, Brittany," he said. "Let's get our partnership established."

"I think it is," she said and shrugged. "Now, what's on your mind this morning?" She looked up from her coffee to see a somber expression on Emilio's face. It was gone in a flash, but she wondered if something about Parker had disturbed him.

"There's something I want to discuss with you," Emilio said.

In the outside light, his sexy, bedroom eyes looked more green than ever and she had a difficult time concentrating on anything else. He withdrew a paper and handed it to her, his fingers lightly brushing hers, yet the contact was volatile. She knew her desire built daily and she tried to quell it, but failed most of the time.

Trying to focus on what Emilio wanted, she unfolded the paper and scanned the contents, to find a résumé by a chef from Brazil.

"And why are you showing me this?"

"You have an excellent chef, but it might be good to have two. You have a fine staff of cooks and a good sous-chef, but this way, you would have two very special, world-class chefs."

Instantly, she bristled and thought that Emilio was stepping in to run things after little more than a week with Brittany Beach.

Trying to control her annoyance with him, she shook her head. "Thanks, but I don't think so. There has to be one person in charge in the kitchen. My chef isn't going to want to share the task. He's very territorial."

The Silhouette Reader Service™ — Here's how it works:

Accepting your 2 free books and 2 free gifts places you under no obligation to buy anything. You may keep the books and gifts and return the shipping statement marked "cancel." If you do not cancel, about a month later we'll send you 6 additional books and bill you just $3.80 each in the U.S. or $4.47 each in Canada, plus 25¢ shipping & handling per book and applicable taxes if any.* That's the complete price and — compared to cover prices of $4.50 each in the U.S. and $5.25 each in Canada — it's quite a bargain! You may cancel at any time, but if you choose to continue, every month we'll send you 6 more books which you may either purchase at the discount price or return to us and cancel your subscription.

*Terms and prices subject to change without notice. Sales tax applicable in N.Y. Canadian residents will be charged applicable provincial taxes and GST. Credit or debit balances in a customer's account(s) may be offset by any other outstanding balance owed by or to the customer. Please allow 4 to 6 weeks for delivery. Offer available while quantities last.

If offer card is missing write to: The Silhouette Reader Service, 3010 Walden Ave., P.O. Box 1867, Buffalo, NY 14240-1867

BUSINESS REPLY MAIL

FIRST-CLASS MAIL   PERMIT NO. 717   BUFFALO, NY

POSTAGE WILL BE PAID BY ADDRESSEE

SILHOUETTE READER SERVICE
3010 WALDEN AVE
PO BOX 1867
BUFFALO NY 14240-9952

NO POSTAGE
NECESSARY
IF MAILED
IN THE
UNITED STATES

Play the

Lucky
Hearts
Game

and get...
2 FREE BOOKS *and*
2 FREE MYSTERY GIFTS...
YOURS to KEEP!

yes! I have scratched off the silver card.
Please send me my *2 FREE BOOKS* and
2 FREE mystery GIFTS. I understand that I
am under no obligation to purchase any books
as explained on the back of this card.

Scratch Here!
then look below to see
what your cards get you...
2 Free Books & 2 Free
Mystery Gifts!

326 SDL ENUL   225 SDL ENNA

FIRST NAME   LAST NAME

ADDRESS

APT.#   CITY

STATE/PROV.   ZIP/POSTAL CODE   (S-D-08/07)

Twenty-one gets you
2 FREE BOOKS and
2 FREE MYSTERY GIFTS!

Twenty gets you
2 FREE BOOKS!

Nineteen gets you
1 FREE BOOK!

TRY AGAIN!

"Wait before you rush to a hasty decision on this," Emilio urged in a mild voice, but she could feel the clash of wills. She suspected he was struggling to stay patient and pleasant with her about doing what he wanted.

He sat back in his rattan chair with his long legs stretched out. He looked as fully in charge as her brother Parker had earlier this morning.

"What will you do if Angier Lougee leaves you, particularly with short notice?" Emilio asked. "It happens."

"I'll face that when it occurs, which it may never."

"If you have two chefs, you won't have to worry about losing one," Emilio persisted, leaning forward and resting his elbows on his knees while he focused an intent, steady stare on her that merely increased her anger. "Brittany Beach will gain a splendid reputation for its fare because you'll have more than one expert and more imagination at work here. This man has a marvelous reputation." He paused to let her think about it.

The idea held no appeal for her, and she shook her head. "Can you imagine two in charge in one kitchen? That's bad enough in a home," she said. "No, I definitely don't want a second chef."

"You're making a hasty decision," Emilio insisted. "Listen to me. Two chefs are not a problem," he said with as much assurance as if she had capitulated. "Here's what we can do."

"You have this all worked out," she said and this time she couldn't keep the sharpness out of her voice.

"Stop being angry with me and listen," he said. "We put Angier in charge. We pay Remigio Tiago, the chef I want to hire, the most money. Everyone is happy."

"Until Angier discovers that Remigio makes the highest wages. Then he'd walk on us."

"How will he ever find out? Remigio isn't throwing it in his face. I won't tell him and neither will you. No one else will know. Angier will never be aware that Remigio gets paid more. We'll hire Remigio with the stipulation that Angier is in charge. Angier remains the executive chef."

"And you think your chef will go for this?"

"I'm sure he will."

"It's crazy, Emilio!" she exclaimed, throwing up her hands. "Angier is touchy about his kitchen. And believe me, it is *his* kitchen. He has it arranged the way he wants."

"I think Remigio can go along with that. I'll make it worth his while and he'll understand about Angier."

She looked around to find Emilio's gaze drifting languidly over her or lingering on her breasts, and she tingled from head to toe. Her heartbeat raced, and she fought the taunting memories of his hot kisses and momentarily forgot chefs. When she realized silence had grown and a faint smile hovered on Emilio's face, she shifted her thoughts to their conversation.

"Make Remigio the second sous-chef and we alternate their schedules so the sous-chefs don't work at the same time," Emilio answered without hesitation. For all she knew, he had already made arrangements with Remigio. She faced the fact that part of her stubborn refusal and her annoyance was because she had dealt with her control-freak brothers all her life and she suspected Emilio was one, too.

Trying to keep an open mind, she drew a deep breath and thought about Emilio's arguments.

"Are you taking over my life, plus fifty percent?" she asked bluntly.

One dark eyebrow arched and he leaned closer. "How I wish I could take over your life. And maybe your fifty percent, too, but no, I'm not in either case. If you don't want it, I'm not pushing this on you. I'm presenting my case because I think this will be better for both of us. Actually, a good deal for Angier, too. If you can't tolerate it, say so," Emilio said disarmingly, smiling at her and waving his hand as if he didn't care in the least what she decided.

"You bluff better than my brothers. They can't blithely deny their interest in something when they really want it."

"I mean what I say," he said and leaned back while he watched her. His green eyes looked guileless, but she didn't think Emilio was nearly as unconcerned as he acted. She thought about what he wanted and what he'd suggested.

"It has possibilities," she admitted. "Maybe. I want to think about it."

"Great. Read Remigio's background and training and experience. You'll see you'll be getting an exceptional chef. We'll have a much stronger position and more to offer customers."

She realized Emilio had a strong argument. At the same time, a stubborn streak in her screamed to stay in complete control and say no. Now was the time to assert herself. If she yielded now, it might be more difficult the next time they disagreed.

He leaned forward. "With both these master chefs we can have a fantastic menu. I've already done this at El Diablo. I don't ever want to be caught without an executive chef."

"You filled in last Sunday rather well, yourself."

"Grilling—that's simple. I don't concoct blue-ribbon recipes and mouth-watering dishes. Remember, if he doesn't work out, we can always get rid of Remigio."

"Let me think about it," she said.

"Fine. I don't want to pressure you, but chefs who are really first-rate, are snapped up quickly. And they aren't available often. This is an excellent chance to get him."

She smiled. "So you are pressuring me to make a decision right now," she said.

He brushed tendrils of hair away from her face. His touch

was feather-light, yet as always, he stirred tingles with every contact. "Do what you want," he said, smiling at her.

"I have some orders to sign," she said, standing to go to her desk. In minutes, she was bent over a stack of papers, trying to concentrate, but unable to stop thinking about Emilio, who worked quietly at the table only feet away from her desk.

She realized instead of growing accustomed to having him around and less susceptible to him, she was doing the opposite.

That afternoon at three o'clock, she found Emilio in the kitchen going over the menu with the executive chef. As soon as he saw her, Emilio left Angier and joined her.

"Were you looking for me?"

"I'm going to my condo."

"I'll go out with you because I was going back to El Diablo," he said, turning to walk with her. They left together, stepping outside into sweltering late afternoon heat that made her think of a quick dip in the pool at her condo.

In the parking lot, he placed his hand on her arm. "Until later," he said and brushed a kiss across her lips.

"If our staff see you do that, you'll start wild rumors."

"I imagine the wild rumors are already flying," Emilio said with amusement sparking in his green eyes. "Until tonight."

He was gone then, striding to his car to climb inside and drive away before she had the door closed as she sat in her black car. She drove out of the lot, remembering his mouth on hers, recalling his hot kisses. Her reactions to him were instant and intense. They talked over an hour nearly every night now after they both went home from work. She'd been to a gallery with him, had him at her place, spent hours with him at work and outside of work.

As she drove home, she continued to think about him. She liked his company and could talk freely to him. She could depend on him in a crunch at Brittany Beach. He was sexy beyond any man she'd ever known. Was she falling in love with Emilio?

In her quiet condo, she went for a brief swim, glad to see the empty pool. As she enjoyed the cool water and exercise, she thought about a second chef and decided Emilio's arguments were valid. Did she want to let him get his way so quickly and easily? That was the big question that plagued her because he was another take-charge male.

She splashed as she floated on her back and wondered if she really had any choice to make. She suspected he was going to get his way. Giving up, she resolved to agree to his suggestion and see how it worked out. Emilio could deal with the change. She flipped over and swam laps, remembering how Brooke never did like to swim, wondering if her twin would ever change.

After a few minutes, Brittany went inside to bathe and dress.

After her bath, she studied her clothes. She knew what Emilio liked and what was sexy to him and turned him on. Indecision racked her and she picked first one outfit and then another before tossing aside caution and selecting a hot-pink shirt and hot-pink skirt and pink high-heeled sandals.

Seven

It was eleven that night before Brittany turned around in the bar to find Emilio lounging against the doorjamb while he watched her.

He walked over to her. "Hi. Think I can have a dance?"

"I don't seem to be needed in any particular place right now so, yes, you can," she replied.

He took her hand and led her to the lounge dance floor and turned her toward him. Dressed in brown slacks and tan shirt, he was as handsome as ever. Black locks of hair fell over his forehead. It was the searing need in his crystal eyes that stirred her own longing.

Wordlessly, they began to dance and the air between them sparked with fire. She knew she was wearing a sexy outfit, dancing a hot, Latin number that meant moving her body in an enticing manner. Tonight, she wanted to be appealing to him. Desire burned a steady, hot flame in her.

Was she ready to throw consequences to the wind? She knew she already had. As she danced around him, she watched him and their surroundings vanished.

Her world narrowed to the flashing lights, a pounding beat and the sexy male moving his hips and long legs and watching her with that devouring look that made her feel as if she were the most desirable woman on earth.

When the dance ended, he took her hand and they left the dance floor and headed toward a table. As they moved through the crowd, she noticed Juan, one of the waitstaff, step into the lounge and look all around and she withdrew her hand from Emilio's. "I think I'm wanted," she said, hurrying to the door and waving at Juan. The minute she walked up to him, he began to talk.

"Someone swung open a door and hit Hector. He's lost consciousness and Luiz called an ambulance."

"Let's go see," Emilio said from behind her. Taking her arm, they hurried after Juan, who led the way to the kitchen where Hector lay on the floor with his eyes open and a compress on his forehead. Waitstaff and chefs were clustered around him and moved back to give Brittany and Emilio room.

"I'm okay," Hector insisted when Brittany knelt beside him. "Cancel the ambulance. I don't need one."

"I know, but you should still get checked out by professionals," Brittany said, concerned about him even though it was reassuring to have him say he was all right. "Lie still until they get here." She glanced up at Emilio, who had called 911, and she heard him tell them to turn the siren off when they entered the Brittany Beach drive and to come around to the back to the kitchen door.

He clicked off and looked at Brittany. "I'll take you to the hospital when Hector goes."

"I got knocked out," Hector grumbled. "I'll be all right."

"Let them look you over to make sure," Brittany said. "I insist and we'll cover any charges the insurance doesn't."

"I'll wait outside for the ambulance," Emilio said and left.

When the paramedics arrived, the time seemed to move slowly as they took Hector's vital signs and checked him over and talked to Brittany. Finally, Hector got to his feet and it was agreed that the ambulance wasn't needed, that Brittany and Emilio would take Hector to the emergency room.

It was almost two in the morning when they left Hector at his home with his wife and Emilio drove Brittany to her condo.

"Come inside and have a drink," she said as he parked in front of her door.

"You won't have to ask twice," he said, getting out and striding around the car to help her out.

In minutes, they had on soft music as they sat in her back room. Emilio had a beer and she had pop and she had kicked off her shoes. "Once again, thanks for your help," she said.

"Sure. I'm glad he wasn't hurt badly."

"I wouldn't have been able to sleep if he hadn't gotten checked by a doctor, even though he didn't think it was necessary at all."

"I'm sure his wife agreed with you," Emilio said. "Now right before that happened, I remember dancing with you," he said, his voice getting deeper. He reached over to take her drink from her hand. "I liked that. How about another dance?"

"There's not much room…."

He stood and set aside his beer, taking her hand to lead her into her kitchen, where only a small light burned. "You can hear the music in here," he said, pulling her into his arms to slow dance.

She moved with him, relaxing and forgetting the problems of the evening. Her awareness of Emilio became more intense. His warm, hard body pressed against her. He held her close.

Desire ignited and she wrapped her arms around his neck to hold him while they swayed slowly.

They danced two dances and then he leaned back to look into her eyes. Her heart slammed against her ribs. She could feel his desire, white-hot, mirroring her own feelings, and then he lowered his head to kiss her.

The minute her lips pressed against his, her insides clenched. His tongue plunged into her mouth and stroked her. Bending over her, he kissed her deeply. His tongue explored her mouth as if he would devour her. And she wanted him to.

Her desire raged and she ached to have no barrier between them, to touch and kiss and caress him. Healthy and strong, he made her burn with longing, and she wanted to discover his powerful, male body.

She had no idea how long they stood kissing. Soft music played in the background, but she was barely aware of it.

Emilio picked her up, holding her in his arms as he turned to carry her to her bedroom, where he set her on her feet and switched on a small table lamp that shed a faint glow.

She wrapped her arms around his neck and stood on tiptoe to kiss him again.

In a few minutes, she leaned back and tugged his shirt out of his slacks. Her fingers fumbled with the buttons at his throat, twisting them free. He brushed away her hands and yanked his shirt over his head, tossing it aside. She looked up into his smoldering gaze that was as sexy as everything else about him. And then her attention lowered to his muscled chest and she ran her hands across him while they kissed.

He slipped off her top, and she had to raise her arms to get free of it. She wore nothing under it and he inhaled, making his chest expand.

Flames of desire filled his eyes while he cupped her breasts in his large, tanned hands. "Beautiful," he whispered. "So beautiful."

Closing her eyes in pleasure, she gasped and clung to his muscled forearms.

He leaned down and his tongue encircled her nipple, hot and wet, making her tremble. Desire pooled low in her, a primitive craving for him. She moaned with relish while exquisite sensations streaked from his kisses. For a few minutes, she simply clung to him and drowned in the kisses and caresses he showered on her.

His thumbs circled her nipples slowly, as lightly as a feather, yet incredibly tantalizing, driving her wild with need.

As torment built, she ran her hands over his chest again, enjoying the bulge of muscles and his strength. She tangled her fingers in his mat of black, curly chest hair and then slid one hand along the column of his neck. Tangling her fingers in his thick hair, she kissed him hungrily, wanting more of him by the minute.

Her hands slid low to unfasten his slacks and let them drop away. She hooked her thumbs in his low-cut briefs. His thick rod bulged out of them, hard and ready for her, a black mat of short curls surrounding his ample endowment. Watching him, she slowly peeled down his briefs and he stepped out of them. His thighs were muscled, covered in a sprinkling of dark curls that were a tantalizing roughness against the smoothness of her legs.

She knelt to caress him and lick him, slowly sliding her tongue along his throbbing shaft. Groaning, he wound his fingers in her hair while he stood with his legs slightly spread.

"Brittany," he whispered.

Slowly, she ran her tongue over him while one hand went between his legs to stroke him, to tease and stir him as he did her. Her other hand slid over his hard bottom. His body was as solid as granite, ready and magnificent.

With another groan, he reached beneath her arms and pulled her up. When they looked into each other's eyes, she could see her own intense craving mirrored there. He drew her into his tight embrace, kissing her hard and leaning over her, his erection thrusting against her while she clung to him.

"I want you more than I've ever dreamed of wanting anyone," she whispered between the kisses she showered on him.

When his arms tightened, his kiss deepened and her heart surged.

His hands unfastened her skirt to let it fall around her ankles. While they kissed, she kicked off her shoes. His hot gaze played thoroughly over her, lingering on her breasts. When his dark hands slipped lower to take the straps of her thong in his fingers and peel it off, she stepped out of it.

Standing again, he placed his hands on her hips and held her away while his eyes traveled slowly over every inch of her. "First, I look," he whispered in a rasp. "Next, I touch and feel and then last, I kiss every inch." She shook, wanting him and wanting to do the same to him.

"You're gorgeous, fantastic!" he exclaimed, his gaze still drifting so slowly over her while his fingers skimmed lightly across her breasts and then lower, over her belly.

She cried out with pleasure as he caressed her.

She started to do the same to him once again, but he yanked the covers back on her bed, picked her up and placed her on it. Moving beside her, he held her close against his hard length while his other hand roamed over her.

Clinging to him, she let one hand drift over his smooth, muscled back. "I want you, Emilio," she whispered. "Now," she urged.

"Soon. Not yet. I want you more passionate."

"I can't be! Love me," she exclaimed.

Ending their conversation, his mouth covered hers. His hand slid along her hip and upper leg and then between her legs. With a cry that was muffled by his kiss, she thrust her hips against him.

He shifted, moving between her legs and his dark head dipped lower, while his tongue went where his fingers had been.

Hot and wet, his tongue circled her feminine spot and she cried out, arching higher for him with need exploding in her. His tongue drove her wild, stroking her, building her torment and pleasure.

"Emilio! Love me!" she cried out, her hands reaching for his thick shaft. "I want you now!" she cried and bit her lip. Her eyes were squeezed shut and sensation rocked her.

Finally, he raised to look at her. "Do you have protection?"

When she shook her head, he pushed her aside, getting up to find his discarded trousers.

As he returned, she drank in the sight of his muscled, lean body and long legs. He was sexy, ready for love. He retrieved a packet from his billfold and climbed back on the bed.

When she shifted and spread her legs, he moved between them. His gaze drifted slowly over her and his fingers played with her.

"You're the most beautiful woman I've known," he said. "And the sexiest."

"I don't believe you, but I like to hear you say it," she whispered. "Come here." She held her arms up to him, longing to kiss him. "I want you inside me."

His eyes darkened as he inhaled deeply and paused. While she drew her fingers along his thighs, he put on the protection and then he lowered himself, the tip of his shaft pressing against her.

When he kissed her, she wrapped her long legs around him and her slender arms around his neck to hold him close. Eagerly, she ran her hands over the curve of his bottom and the back of his hard thighs.

He filled her slowly and she felt as if she would burst from his thickness, yet she wanted him and she moved her hips, meeting his thrusts with her own. She knew he was struggling for control, trying to increase her pleasure and desire, but she was driven with a primitive desperation.

She held him with her legs and stroked him, trying to drive him to the point where he had taken her, where his control was gone and the ultimate release was the only thing that would satisfy him.

With a sound deep in his throat, he kissed her as he filled her slowly again, moving with a restraint that built her need to pure torment.

Finally, his control was gone and he pumped into her, moving hard and fast and she matched him.

She spun into an erotic world of passion and intimacy. They rocked together, building toward the climax.

"Emilio!" she cried, unaware of calling his name, her hips moving frantically with his, while need pounded like her racing heartbeat.

"Brittany!" he gasped. He thrust into her, taking her to a brink and then she cried out and climaxed, feeling spasms rock him as he climaxed with her.

Her pulse roared and rapture blossomed, exploding with her release. She cried out again, clinging to him, feeling his strong back that was covered in sweat. They both gasped for breath.

"Don't stop," she whispered, wanting to prolong the ecstasy, wanting this moment to last when they were one and he was hers and she was his. For now, life was bliss.

As he slowed, he kissed her. She held him tightly, relishing his body, his sexiness, his manhood. "I could kiss you all night," she whispered, running her hand over his smooth back.

He showered kisses on her temple and finally he slowed and let his weight rest on her. He turned on his side, taking her with him and, blissfully, she gazed at him.

"So sexy," he whispered. "I'm lucky to have found you, Brittany." A satisfied look passed between them. She framed his face with her hands and kissed him tenderly. When she raised her head, he rolled onto his back and she slid beside him, placing her head on his shoulder while he held her close and their legs entwined.

"Things changed between us tonight," he replied solemnly, and she smiled.

"At the moment, it's a wonderful change."

He studied her and brushed a kiss on her forehead. "I want to hold you all night. You set me on fire. You're beautiful."

"You're rather appealing, yourself," she said, running her index finger along his jaw, feeling the faint growth of stubble.

"I want to be with you, looking at you, kissing you, making love to you," he said lazily.

"Help yourself," she said and she raised up to run her hand lightly over his chest. "Look all you want."

As she caressed him, his eyes darkened. She traced her fingers across his flat, washboard belly, going lower and moving to his thighs, watching as he stirred.

"Two can do that," he said, his voice getting deep. Releasing her, he stepped off the bed and picked her up. "Ready for a warm shower?"

"I'm ready for anything with you," she said, feeling bubbly, desire reawakening in her.

He set her on her feet in her shower and turned on the water, then wrapped his arms around her and kissed her hungrily.

As warm water spilled over her, she rubbed against him, letting her hands slide along his sides.

Desire was a hot flame, making her move her hips against his. His shaft thrust against her, hard and ready.

They soaped each other and rubbed away the soap and finally he turned off the water while they dried and he pulled the towel slowly and lightly across her taut nipples, the friction a sweet torment. Next, he slipped it between her legs to cause another fiery friction. She gasped and wrapped her arms around him to kiss him.

He picked her up to carry her into the bedroom back to bed, where he held her close. "This is the best night ever," he said in his deep voice that was a rumble against her ear.

Raising up, she leaned forward to let her nipples touch his chest and she rubbed lightly against him.

He toyed with her hair and watched her while she ran her fingers slowly up the inside of his thigh and leaned down to rub her nipples against his belly this time. She was getting aroused, feeling his warm body and fueling her rising need. Sex with him had been great—as she had expected.

Suddenly, he rolled her over on her back and he straddled her, placing his hands on both sides of her face as he gazed into her eyes. Her heart leaped. "Are we going to make love for hours?" she asked.

"I plan to," he said and then leaned the last few inches to cover her mouth with his.

She wound her arm around his neck and held him tightly. His hands were everywhere, sliding over her, caressing her, rubbing her and the spiral started again.

In minutes, she was gasping, wanting him inside her more than before, shocked by her own need that was compelling beyond what she would have believed possible.

And then he retrieved another condom. He stretched on his back and settled her on his thick shaft, plunging into her as she moved on him. While he was inside her, hot and hard, his hand played with her nipple and the other hand rubbed her feminine bud. She moved faster, need building, sensations bombarding her from his hands and his erection and his loving.

She squeezed her eyes closed and rocked on him, the exquisite torment growing until release burst inside her and she climaxed.

He pounded into her, holding her on him while he climaxed.

The roaring of her pulse deafened her. Sex with Emilio was better than she had hoped, lustier and more satisfying, yet each kiss and caress forged a link in a chain that bound her heart to him irrevocably. She knew she could be plunging headlong into heartbreak, but at the moment, she didn't care.

Finally exhausted and covered in perspiration, she sprawled over him. "You're fantastic, Emilio."

"Your gorgeous, sexy body is impossible to resist," he said, playing with her hair. He rolled her beside him and held her close while he smoothed her hair away from her face. "We're good together, Brittany."

Warm pleasure filled her and she held him tightly, feeling their hearts beating together while she rubbed her cheek against him. "I'm happy."

"Great," he said. "I hope you always are," he added and she looked up, hearing a strange note of concern in his voice. She wondered what was bothering him.

"Sounds perfect," she said happily, not wanting to interrupt their moment.

They made love through the early hours of the morning until finally, Emilio climbed out of bed and headed for the shower. "I have to go home, but I'd rather stay here in bed with you."

She rolled on her side to look at him. He was virile, naked and aroused.

"I don't think you're going anywhere right now," she said in a sultry voice, moving sensuously on the bed. He inhaled, as his gaze drifted over her and he came back to pull her into his arms and it was another hour before he got up and found his cell phone to call and tell his general manager that he wouldn't arrive at El Diablo until late in the day.

When he returned to bed, he took her into his arms. She twisted to look at him and wrap her arm around his neck. "I'm glad you're staying."

Eight

They spent the morning making love and finally, by mid-afternoon, Emilio insisted he had to leave. She walked to the door with him, where he turned to kiss her one last time. When he released her, she looked up at him.

"Brittany, last night, today, it was all the very best ever," he said, sounding sincere.

Her heart jumped and she looked into his unfathomable green eyes. He was somber, looking intently at her and she wondered what was going through his thoughts.

"You look worried, Emilio. Is something wrong?"

He gazed at her in silence, while something flickered in the depths of his eyes and she realized she might have been intrusive with her question.

"Am I treading on something private?" Brittany asked, wishing she hadn't quizzed him.

He placed his hand on her shoulder. "You can ask anything

you want. In some ways, I feel closer to you than to anyone else I've ever known," he said, and she drew a deep breath. She rested her palm against his cheek.

"That's the nicest thing you could possibly say," she said softly. "That's even better than the picture you gave me."

He shrugged. "We've gotten to be friends, Brittany. I know I can count on you."

"Yes, you can," she said, "but don't look so unhappy about it."

He smiled at her and slid his hand behind her head to pull her to him to kiss her. She put her arms around his neck to return his kiss, her heart beating fast because his words had made her feel a stronger bond than ever with him. Finally, he released her.

"I'm not unhappy. Just the opposite," he said, flashing one of his spectacular smiles. "Now I better go," he said. "But I hate to. I'll call and we can talk," he said. "I'm going to miss you terribly."

Nodding, she blew him a kiss and he headed to his car.

Emilio drove to his condo and walked out on the terrace and cast his attention into the distance without seeing the beach or ocean. Instead, he saw Brittany's lush body over his, her tongue stroking him, her mouth raised to his, but then he thought about the past hours and how she had given totally to him. Before, she had trusted him with her business. In the past two nights, she'd trusted him with her body. And he had deceived her in business. He knotted his fists in frustration.

For several years, Jordan and he had fought with the Garrison men. If Emilio and Jordan could wipe out the Garrison competition, they would. They intended to cut into it as much as possible. And when he'd gone after Brittany Beach, Emilio had thought it a mere extension of all he'd already dealt with in the Garrison family. Brittany had been ripe for picking and he had pursued her restaurant.

He was caught in a trap of his own making, Emilio realized. He had violated her trust. And she had given him her trust—the most a woman could give a man—complete intimacy.

If he admitted the truth to her, she would hate him. And if he didn't tell her and she discovered it—which she would when she finally broke the news about her partner to her family—she would despise him.

Wind blew locks of his hair as he stared out to the horizon. He knew he was ruined, no matter what happened. He didn't know if confession would be one degree better than letting her discover the Garrison-Jefferies feud from someone else.

Emilio clenched his fist again in frustration. There was no good way out of his problem. He thought about Brittany in his arms, pressed against him, beautiful, sexy, trusting.

What a bastard he'd been! He couldn't blame her for hating him and the thought pained him. It surprised him how badly the deception hurt and how much it worried him. Was he beginning to care for her? Really care in a manner he'd never known before in his life? He had never gotten closely involved with any of the women who had been in his life. It had been lust and excitement. This caring was something new and he didn't like it because he hurt.

Brittany was important to him. He shared interests with her. She was sexy, fun and he could trust her with his secrets. She wasn't interested in his money. She was frank and truthful and dependable.

He was into it now and it was only a matter of time until everything blew up in his face. Then what would he do? Finding no solution, he turned and went inside, preparing to go to work.

By the time he was in the car, his thoughts were on the past hours of lovemaking with Brittany and his spirits had lifted. Forgetting his worries, Emilio drove toward SoBe and El Diablo. He wanted Brittany and couldn't wait until he could see her again.

He'd been infatuated many times, but he didn't remember being consumed by desire for someone before. Brittany was special and different.

Last night and this morning had been the best ever. Whatever that chemistry between them, it was unparalleled and fantastic. He was getting aroused thinking about her and he wanted her right then. He ached to hold her, kiss her and make love with her again. With a groan, he realized he would have to go hours before he saw her and even more time before she would be naked in his arms.

As he turned into the parking lot and drove to the back of El Diablo, he swore because Jordan's car was in the lot. Right now, Emilio didn't care to see his brother.

He climbed out of his car and into his office, where Jordan sat writing in a tablet.

"Well, hello. I thought you'd be here half an hour ago." Jordan tilted his head to study him. "You look like the weight of the world is on your shoulders."

"Actually, no. I'm doing fine," Emilio lied, wanting to avoid discussing his dilemma with Jordan, who looked cool and casual in a blue shirt and chinos and deck shoes.

"So how's business—particularly Brittany Beach?" Jordan asked, still scrutinizing his brother.

"Business at both Brittany Beach and here is booming."

"I heard when we had the storm, that Brittany Beach was one of the places to be in SoBe."

"Right. It was packed until the wee hours of the morning."

"Her brothers still don't know, do they? When they find out, you'll have war. Of course, what could they expect? Send a flighty baby sister out who doesn't know squat and someone will have her skirts over her head before she knows what happened," Jordan said lightly and grinned.

While he tried to curb his temper, Emilio's insides tightened and he gripped the arms of his chair. "She's not flighty, Jordan. I misjudged her, and so have they. Actually, she's a damn good businesswoman."

"Uh-oh. Sounds like a man enveloped in lust. I can't believe Brittany Garrison has any business sense."

"She does. I'm telling you that in the cold light of morning," Emilio said seriously. "I misjudged her because she had the embezzlement and she accepted my help so quickly. She's shrewd about the restaurant business and the night of the storm, she managed quite well," Emilio insisted, wishing Jordan would go and take his annoying opinions with him.

"So it may be more difficult than you expected for you to take the whole thing away from her."

"I'm not doing that," Emilio said flatly, and Jordan frowned.

"Your feelings for Brittany Garrison come before the Jefferies' interests?" Jordan asked with surprise and annoyance in his tone.

"That's my business, Jordan," Emilio snapped.

"If you put her before our interests, you're a traitor to the family."

"Dammit! You take that back."

"You're siding with a Garrison. Deny that one."

"Did you want to see me about something?" Emilio asked, clamping his jaw closed and trying to hang on to his temper. He glared at his brother while Jordan glowered and Emilio tensed, wondering if they were going to come to blows. "What do you want?"

"Really, nothing. Only to see how it was going with El Diablo and with Brittany Beach." He stood. "I'm going because I can see that I'm not wanted, but I'm telling you, bro, you better dump her and work your fifty percent from afar. Don't let her come between us. I don't want to have anything to do with a Garrison."

Emilio wanted to jump over the desk and take a swing at Jordan. Instead, he controlled his temper and glared at his brother as he stood.

"Those Garrison men are going to be madder than hell when they find out what's happened," Jordan persisted. "And when she discovers how much you deceived her, she's going to be angry, herself."

"Go to hell, Jordan."

"Brittany Garrison isn't for you." Jordan turned and strode out of the office, slamming the door behind him.

Emilio swung his fist through the air, wishing he could hit something. Frustrated and angry, he decided to go to the gym for a workout.

Two hours of exercise didn't change his grim outlook. He was steeped in deception with Brittany and he didn't see any way out of it, except to confess the truth to her. This soon in their relationship, he didn't want to do that. At this point, he was certain he would lose her.

And he hated to see Jordan leave his office in a huff. Emilio swore out loud. He didn't want to drive a wedge between Jordan and himself. His thoughts jumped back to Brittany.

Tonight, he would be with her and eagerness made him forget everything else and stop worrying about confessing to her. For now, he wasn't going to worry about it. Tonight, he would take time and savor every moment with her.

The damnable Garrison Sunday dinners were a threat. Every time the Garrisons were together, chances of Brittany discovering his deceit shot higher. Maybe soon she would care enough for him to forgive him when she learned the truth.

Yeah, right, he said to himself, shaking his head. He could imagine her fury that wasn't going to end with forgiveness. He knew he postponed the inevitable, but he wasn't ready to lose her.

He went by his home that night to shower and change. He

dressed in gray slacks and a navy shirt. After combing his hair, he left for Brittany Beach.

By the time he walked into the restaurant, it was ten o'clock. Drums pounded out a slow, sensual rhythm in the lounge and dancers gyrated in the semidarkness. Emilio peered through the flashing lights for a glimpse of Brittany.

Then he spotted her in the dining room and his pulse jumped. Her short skirts and clinging silk tops turned him on— actually, the body they revealed was what turned him on. Tonight, she had another outfit that hugged her slender hips and flat belly and he ached to peel her right out of it.

Her top was a blue halter that ended high above her midriff and revealed a bare middle, shoulders and back. She was hot and he could look at her forever, but he wanted far more to kiss and taste and caress her as he had last night.

He crossed the room to her, walking up behind her. Emilio didn't want to startle her, but she was turned away from him. Her long hair was looped and clipped on the back of her head and he wanted to reach out and take that clip out of her hair and let it fall over her shoulders, which he would do as soon as they were alone. Soon, she would be naked in his arms in his bed. Just as quickly as he could get her out of Brittany Beach and back to his place.

"Brittany," he said softly, reaching to take her arm and turn her to face him. His pulse raced and he felt as if he had waited months for this moment, instead of merely hours.

"Hi!" she exclaimed, flashing him a warm smile that made his heart jump.

"You haven't seen my place. Everything's going smoothly here. Let me show you where I live," he said. "Can you leave with me now?"

"Give me time to tell people," she said, giving him an eager, heated look that sped his heartbeat even more.

In minutes, they were in his car heading for his condo, which was the penthouse of a high-rise oceanfront building. As soon as he closed the door behind them, he pulled her into his embrace. Brittany flung her arms around his neck as if she hadn't seen him in years.

While they kissed, he lifted her up into his strong arms.

Brittany was oblivious to where he carried her, and barely conscious of the bed beneath her when he lowered her and stretched out beside her to kiss her.

She pushed against him and raised up. "Wait a minute. Slow down, here. I've never been in your place before. I want to see where I am."

"I got carried away," he replied in a rough voice, caressing her nape.

"I think I'm the one that got carried away—to bed," she said with amusement and they laughed with each other.

"I'm glad you're here," he said. "I'll show you around and then I'll have my way with you," he teased, standing and offering her his hand, which she took as she stepped off the bed.

"I can't think of anything more delightful than for you to have your way with me, unless I get to have my way with you," she retorted, and he draped his arm across her shoulders.

"All right. Do you want the grand tour now?"

"Of course," she said, looking around his large bedroom that held a king-size brass bed. She walked about, looking at his shelves with books, pictures and trophies for swimming and golf. She turned to face him. "You have swimming trophies. No wonder I couldn't beat you across the pool. You're a pro."

"I'm not a pro. Those are high school and college trophies. Just admit it. I can swim faster than you can."

"You could last week. Maybe not this week," she said with haughty disdain.

He grinned. "We may have to go for a midnight swim and settle this again."

"Don't be so smug. You've won trophies and I'm a mere amateur."

"Darlin', you're the most adorable amateur I've ever seen and if it makes you happy to win, next time, I'll throw the race," he said, walking over to her.

"Don't you dare! I win on my own merits or not at all," she snapped, knowing they were teasing and it was all in jest. "Oh, well. There are other things we can do where I can come out on top."

"You definitely come out on top in some ways I can think about. Want me to show you?" he asked and she shook her head.

"Not yet. You said that you'd show me your condo."

"You're in my bedroom," he said. She looked around at the polished hardwood floor, the brown leather furniture and the teak dresser, a teak desk, shelves with books, bronze statues and framed pictures, a plasma television. Modern art with vivid colors accented the darker tones.

"This room fits you," she said. "And now I'll know how things look when I talk to you on the phone."

He took her arm. "Over there is the bathroom. I'll give you a special tour of it and my shower later," he said and she smiled. He led her outside on his terrace and she gasped at the view. "You can see the lights along the beach and the street below, but beyond that is the ocean, with yachts and boats and, occasionally, the big cruise ships. The view in the day is spectacular. On the other side of the condo, you can see all of SoBe and Miami and a million lights."

"It's fantastic," she said.

"Yes, it is. I've been waiting all day."

She turned to look up at him, knowing he was not talking

about his view. "Wait a few minutes longer and show me around. I'll try to make it worth your time," she said in a sultry voice, flirting with him.

He draped his arm across her shoulders to show her a formal living room that held traditional oak furniture, elegant sofas and chairs. They walked through his dining room, that was equally formal, with a table that would seat twenty.

"Here's where I live," he said next, and she entered a room with contemporary rattan furniture covered in material with earth tones of warm browns and orange. She could see a media room beyond it and then he took her to his kitchen, a cheery yellow-and-white room that held state-of-the-art equipment.

They looked at another bedroom with a king-size teak bed and contemporary furniture in primary colors. As she looked around, he came up behind her to wrap her in his arms and nuzzle her neck.

"Now, you've had the royal tour. I want to do my own touring," he said quietly in a hoarse voice that made her breath catch. He turned her to face him, reaching out to release the clip that held her hair behind her head.

Over two hours later, he stepped out of bed and picked her up. "We'll shower and then have a late snack," he said, smiling at her.

Joy bubbled in her and desire was reawakening. As he carried her across the room, she glanced outside again at the view of a long string of lights far below and then darkness spreading away to infinity. "You have the best view in the world up here."

"Indeed, I do," he said in a husky voice, looking down at her and she forgot outside. She was warm, naked, held against his bare body in his strong embrace. She tightened her arm around his neck and kissed his shoulder.

Stepping into his bathroom, Emilio switched on a light and she looked at a huge black-and-gold, marble-and-glass bathroom.

"This is enormous. You could get lost in here," she said, gazing at a sunken tub, a huge shower and a dressing area.

He stepped into the shower and set her on her feet and she forgot her surroundings, except for the tall, dark-skinned man holding her waist. He ran his fingers lightly across her breasts and she inhaled.

They started with soap and washcloths, but in seconds, the cloths were tossed aside as they kissed and caressed each other's warm, wet bodies.

Eventually, he put on protection, braced himself and picked her up. She wrapped her long legs around him as he settled her on his thick rod and she moved wildly on him.

When she climaxed, she cried his name and sank against him, pleasured and wrapped in his arms. Ecstasy enveloped her. He thrust into her, as release burst in him and his breathing gradually slowed.

Afterward, she slid down to stand. They showered and dried each other before moving back to the bed where he held her close against him until he fell asleep.

Long after his breathing was deep and steady, she raised up to look at him. His dark lashes were feathered above his prominent cheekbones. He had become her partner and then her friend and now her lover. She'd had fun being with him, looking at art, flirting with him, even working together and their phone conversations were great, but now the friendship had deepened for her into something stronger. She knew she was falling in love with him. She wondered how important she really was to him.

She remembered the moment this morning when he said that he felt closer to her than anyone he had ever known. That had been a stunning admission and she couldn't imagine he had told that to any other female. She had thought about it all through the day.

She touched him on his shoulder. "I love you," she whispered, leaning over to brush a kiss so lightly on his mouth.

His arm tightened around her and he held her close. She started to tell him that she was sorry she had awakened him, but then she saw that he still slept, so she snuggled against him and wrapped her arm around his narrow waist to hold him close.

Glancing at the clock, she saw it was only a few hours until sunrise and it was already Sunday morning. Tonight, she faced another family dinner. Each week was a little less stressful than the one before because she had moved further away from the disastrous embezzlement.

It was three in the afternoon before she kissed Emilio goodbye to leave for her own place. Emilio had called a car service to take her home. "I'll see you later tonight," she said. "I have to get this Sunday dinner over with."

"Skip it once."

"I'm tempted, but I think I should go. It's not the same, though, without our dad. Not at all. Mother is having a tough time and she's trying to deal with it," Brittany said. "At least our dinners don't last late."

"Come straight back here," he said, his green eyes intense as he waited for her answer. "I'll want you in my arms again," he added and she nodded.

"I will," she promised. "I'm going to miss you," she said, not yet ready to tell him that she had fallen in love because she didn't expect to hear those words from him.

"You look gorgeous, as usual," he added. "Although it's best when you wear nothing."

Wrinkling her nose at him, she smiled. "I'll call you when I leave Bal Harbour," she said, blowing him a kiss and leaving.

There would be no storm to cut tonight's dinner short and she dreaded the evening. Their mother's drinking was making dinners more tense.

Her impatience grew as they all sat around the table and she had to resist the urge to continually glance at her watch. She tried to make an effort to join in the conversation. Parker, in his usual white shirt and dark tie, looked the authority figure. Brooke was unusually quiet and Brittany once again sensed something amiss with her sister.

"You're quiet tonight," Stephen remarked to Brittany. Turning to him, she shrugged.

"I guess I'm preoccupied. Mother seems worse," Brittany whispered, glancing toward the end of the table.

"She is worse," he replied quietly, and a muscle worked in his jaw. "Lisette is worried sick about her. Mom stumbled and missed a step this week and almost fell. She's okay, but things are getting out of hand."

"Lower your voice," Brittany said.

"You think she'll pay any attention to any of us?" he snapped. "She's already in a stupor."

Brittany glanced at her mother, but all she could feel was relief that Stephen was focused on their mother and he didn't seem to have any knowledge of Emilio.

"How are things going at the Garrison Grand?"

"Fine, but that reminds me of something I wanted to mention to Parker," he said.

Relieved to shift the conversation from her and glad every time a topic came up that had nothing to do with Brittany Beach, she tried to keep focused on the conversations.

"Parker, we need to update some of the decor at the Garrison Grand. It's getting overdue," Stephen said.

"The hotel has to stay first-class," Parker replied. "Wilkins and Tyler did some work for me that was good."

"I've heard Megan Simmons is back in town as a partner at her former interior design firm," Anna said. "Megan's reputation in that field is growing. I'd think all of you would like her work."

"I'll second that recommendation," Brittany added, happy to stay on the subject of the Garrison Grand. "She did the project at Garrison, Inc. headquarters four years ago, Stephen," Brittany added. "Remember?" she asked, certain he did because he and Megan were a couple when Brittany met her.

Looking shocked, Stephen frowned. "Megan's back in town?" he asked Anna and she nodded.

"I didn't know you knew her," Anna said.

"Why don't you call her?" Brittany asked her brother, surprised by Stephen's reaction to Anna's announcement.

"I'll look into the matter," Stephen answered with a clipped tone to his words. Brittany knew her brother and when something flickered in the depths of his brown eyes, she wondered what disturbed him. If it had been Parker, Brittany would have suspected he didn't want others telling him what to do, but Stephen was more receptive. Still, he had a definite hesitation which surprised her because, for a while after Megan disappeared out of Stephen's life, Brittany suspected he was carrying a torch for her. Perhaps she'd been wrong.

Stephen's gaze swung to her and she smiled and looked away, wanting to avoid any close scrutiny, herself. She didn't know what was going on with Stephen, but if he focused on his properties instead of hers, she would be happy.

Parker could hardly take his gaze from Anna. With a smile at Anna, he looked up. "I'd like everyone's attention," he said and glanced around the table again. "I want to make an announcement."

Conversation died, and all of them turned their attention to Parker, except Bonita, who was studying her drink and swirling her glass slightly. As they waited, Brittany couldn't imagine what Parker had on his mind.

His eyes sparkled and she realized she had never seen him look that enthused over any deal he had made. Anna was radiant as she smiled at Parker and he took her hand. "Anna and I are getting married. We decided to marry Saturday afternoon."

There was one second of stunned surprise and then the siblings started talking and asking questions at once. Parker raised his hand for quiet. "Before you quiz us, let me tell you our plans, and then see if you still have something you want to know. This is short notice, so we're not having attendants because the wedding is within days. We'll marry at the Garrison Grand on the beach and then have a party. We'll have announcements sent out tomorrow, but I'm having my secretary call our closest friends. Can all of you be there?"

There were nods and positive replies and Stephen stood and raised his glass. "Here's a toast to the happy couple. Best wishes from all of us for a long and joyful marriage."

Everyone raised their glasses in a salute to Parker and Anna and later, the minute dinner was over, Brittany and Brooke both went to Anna to welcome her into the family again.

It was nine when Brittany finally got away and as soon as she was in her car, she called Emilio to tell him she was on her way.

The second he opened the door to his condo, she walked into his arms.

Clothes were strewn from the door to the bedroom, but she barely noticed. She ran her hands over him as she kissed him and felt as if she had been away from him forever. "I can't believe how much I missed you," she whispered.

They made love through the night and slept for a couple of

hours after the morning sun spilled into his bedroom. Finally, she sat up and dressed.

"Emilio, it's almost eight in the morning! I have to go home and get to Brittany Beach. You've ruined me."

"Are you complaining?" he asked, pulling her into his arms to smile at her. She wound her arms around his neck.

"I don't think so," she said. "Kiss me and I'll see if I have a complaint."

"Gladly," he said, covering her mouth with his. Her heart thudded and she was amazed how she continually wanted him more. He excited her more all the time. Her pulse raced and his kisses melted her and she didn't care if she ever got out of bed or home or to Brittany Beach.

It was two hours later when she rolled over and sat up, pulling the sheet to her chin. "I do have to go now."

"I'll order breakfast sent up from the restaurant next door. You can eat with me," he said, stretching out his long arm for the phone and placing an order. "Now, we shower."

"No way. I'll shower in your guest bathroom," she said and hurried to gather her things. He crossed the room and caught her before she left, turning her into his arms. She saw that he was aroused and she shook her head.

"I have to get out of bed, Emilio," she insisted.

"One kiss. You walk around like that—"

"I'm covered in a sheet, for heaven's sake!"

"I know there's nothing under that sheet except a beautiful, naked woman," he said and kissed her long and hard. Finally, she pushed away and hurried to the shower, closing the door and knowing she would have to resist him again or never get away today.

They ate on his terrace with a view of the ocean and yachts at anchor.

"What a beautiful day," she exclaimed.

"I can only see a beautiful woman," he said, reaching across the table to touch her cheek lightly.

She smiled at him. "This is good."

"Very good," he repeated. "How was the family dinner last night? I never got to ask you."

"Fine. Parker and Anna announced they're marrying Saturday at the Garrison Grand on the beach. Parker is so in love that he's a different person."

"I doubt that," Emilio remarked drily. "Your brother is all business and practical. Falling in love isn't going to change him much or for long."

"You'd be surprised."

"Damned surprised," Emilio replied with such force that she looked up.

"Have you had a conflict with Parker?"

Shrugging, Emilio toyed with his ice water. "Everyone in Miami knows your brother—I should correct that to say every businessman in Miami. Tourists don't know the Garrisons. Now enough about Parker. When do we get to be together again? I have appointments and business at El Diablo today. How about eating a midnight dinner with me tonight here at my condo?"

Feeling giddy with happiness, she laughed. "Midnight supper? Sounds ridiculous, but how can I refuse you?" she asked and lost her appetite for her breakfast at the look in his eyes. Desire flamed while he stood and came around to pull her to her feet. Wrapping his arms around her, he kissed her.

She didn't know how much time passed before she pushed away. "Now I have to go. I'll be with you tonight."

He walked to the elevator with her where he kissed her again and wanted her to come back inside with him, but she said goodbye and left.

She drove straight to Brittany Beach to find the noon crowd already gathering.

* * *

By eight o'clock that night, she had talked to Emilio a dozen times and the midnight dinner had been moved up an hour. As she stood in the dining room, she saw Parker striding across the room toward her. Her first thought was that something had happened to their mother.

Instantly, that concern was replaced. With a frown wrinkling his brow, Parker was charging toward her without looking at anyone except her. He was furious and she could guess why. Parker had discovered Emilio was her partner.

Nine

"I take it something's wrong," Brittany said as Parker walked up to her.

"Yes, it is. We'll talk in your office," he said, looking over her head, gazing around the dining room. She was certain that he'd heard about Emilio and was looking for him.

With her heart drumming, she led the way and as soon as they had her doors closed, she turned to Parker, whose face was red. "I assume you've learned I have a partner," she said, raising her chin.

"Dammit, yes. Stephen wanted to come, but I told him I'd take care of this. He'll probably call you. How the hell could you do this?"

"Don't swear at me, Parker!" she snapped, her anger soaring over his high-handed ways.

"You deserve more than swearing. We've let you keep this restaurant, but you've betrayed us. I want to boot you off and take the place. Then see how well you and your partner do."

"Don't you dare, Parker!" she yelled at him, her temper boiling. "You know if our father were alive, he would never let you evict me!" she yelled. "You leave me alone. This is my business to run as I see fit."

"When you take in the enemy as your partner, that's it."

"What are you talking about, 'the enemy'?"

"You know damn well what I'm talking about!" Parker retorted. "You know the Garrisons and the Jefferies feud like the Hatfields and the McCoys. We've fought those damned Jefferies over more deals than I can count. They've tried to ruin every Garrison thing they can or compete with us and we've been at war with them for the past few years. Our father fought them like crazy."

Stunned, she stared at him while her mind reeled and all her anger drained away. "What are you talking about, Parker?"

Glaring at her, he took a deep breath. "You didn't know that we have a feud with Emilio and Jordan Jefferies?"

"No, I didn't know that," she answered. "What war with the Jefferies?" she asked, beginning to shake.

"I'll be damned, you don't know!" Parker exclaimed and frowned at her. "They compete with us and want to ruin us if they can. They want to build an empire like we have. They try to beat us to buy property that we want. They've used blind trusts and other people representing them and now this? Emilio Jefferies becomes your partner?"

"I didn't know anything about a Garrison-Jefferies history," Brittany said stiffly. She had been deceived by Emilio. He had been after Garrison business. No wonder he had made the suggestion to her and offered his money and help.

What a dupe she had been! On top of that hurt was the knowledge the family didn't bother to keep her informed about things all the others knew.

"I don't know how you could keep from knowing about

them when they've caused us so damned much trouble," Parker grumbled.

"Why didn't any of you tell me?"

"I suppose it didn't seem important."

"I know why," she said bitterly. "You don't think it matters what I know or don't know. Well, I wouldn't have taken him for a partner if I'd been informed. You should tell me what's going on."

"Most things don't involve you or Brittany Beach and you know it. How much percentage did he get?"

"Fifty percent," she admitted, and Parker grimaced as he mouthed a word, but didn't say it aloud.

"A Jefferies has half!" Parker stormed, his frown deepening.

"Keep me informed if you don't want me to do something I shouldn't. What did you expect?"

"Damn well not for you to go out and take in our worst enemy and hand over fifty percent of the restaurant! Damnation, Brittany, if our dad were alive, he'd take the place back from you. We can't take Jefferies' half now. That's his. He's got a Garrison business. I'll bet those Jefferies had a blast celebrating and if you think they didn't split their sides laughing at the deal they put over on you—think again."

Parker's words stabbed like a knife because she knew they were true. She rubbed her forehead. All the nightmare accusations of her family that she was inept, flighty and didn't have business sense—every charge haunted her because she had proved them right.

Angry and hurt, she glared at Parker. "I didn't know, Parker."

"Well, now you know and he's got half of this! Damn, what a fool he's made of you! He better lie low and stay out of my sight. I swear, I'll punch him out. Is he here now?"

"No, he's not and he won't be tonight," she answered.

"That's good for him. He's got half your business. I'm sure he plans to take it all from you. We're not going to let him do that, Brittany."

"I won't let him take my part away from me," she said, knowing that Parker didn't think she was competent enough to stop Emilio.

"Damn straight he won't, but I'm the one who'll see to that. He got half from you and I'll bet he did it easily. Do you have the contract?"

"Of course," she said. "Brandon has the original." She walked around her desk to unlock and open a bottom drawer.

"Brandon?"

"He has to observe client-attorney confidentiality, so don't go yelling at him. He couldn't tell you no matter how badly he wanted to." She withdrew a folder and carried it to Parker. "Did Brandon know about the feud?"

"Yes, I thought all of SoBe, including you, knew it," Parker huffed. "But Brandon couldn't tell you for the same reason he couldn't tell me about your contract with Emilio—attorney-client confidentiality."

"I guess you're right. He was noncommittal, but I sensed disapproval. I figured it was because he knew you wouldn't like me taking in a partner. He suggested I talk it over with you, and I told him I didn't want to."

"That makes me feel better about Brandon. You should've taken his advice."

"I didn't know the reason for it."

"That doesn't matter, Brittany."

"Parker, you don't think I have a brain in my head!" she accused, glaring at her brother, who scowled in return.

"Thank God you had Brandon do the legal work, though," Parker said, ignoring her comment in which she was certain he concurred. "I trust the contract to be okay if he had a part in it, but I still want to see it. I'll have a copy made and get this back to you. What did you get out of the deal?"

"Emilio has a two-million-dollar investment and he'll lend his restaurant expertise," she said stiffly, hurting badly while anger burned. Emilio had deceived her from the start. She'd trusted him as much as a person could trust another and he had violated that trust completely.

"With two million they acquire a Garrison property. Does he know you don't own the land?"

"Yes, but he doesn't know that you would evict me in a flash. He assumes it's a Garrison deal so I'm here to stay."

"Why didn't you come to us if you wanted two million or advice or any other damn thing?"

"My family doesn't exactly work cooperatively with me," she said with sarcasm lacing her voice. "You know you wouldn't have wanted to give me money to put into this and you would have stepped in and taken over. Admit it, Parker. You're just waiting for an excuse far less than this to take Brittany Beach."

"What got into you, to take anyone into your business? Why did you do it?"

"I thought I was doing something that would be good. This place is turning a profit. It's popular and profits increase every single month. I can invest more in it to make it grow." She knew her reason sounded weak, but she was not about to tell Parker about the embezzlement.

"I'll tell you, Brittany, I don't want the Jefferies in our business," Parker said.

"Don't evict me. I have a successful place. When I start to lose money, then we can talk about eviction. Until then, I'll take you to court."

"You'll lose," Parker said.

"I know that, but I'll tie you up and cost Garrison, Inc. money until you'd wished you'd left me alone."

"That's a hell of an attitude!" Parker complained.

"I'm trying to save my restaurant. The one Dad gave me. What about your outlook when it comes to ousting me because I took in a Jefferies, when you didn't tell me you had a feud with them?" she asked in exasperation. "I'll do something about Emilio because I didn't know there was a feud, but you leave me and Brittany Beach alone."

Parker nodded. "All right, but come to me if you want money. Don't go to outsiders. You should've let us put the money into this."

"You know you would have refused," she repeated. "Don't expect me to believe anything else. If I'd known," she said bitterly, "I wouldn't have taken him in. I'll deal with him, though."

"Keep me posted about what you're going to do and what that partner of yours plans," Parker ordered.

"I will," she promised, wondering exactly how she would deal with Emilio.

Parker nodded and thumped the folder with the contract against his leg. "All right, Brittany. Keep in touch."

Feeling numb, she walked with her brother to the front and watched him go outside and talk on his cell phone while he waited for a valet to bring his car. She was certain he was talking to Stephen about meeting to look over her contract with Emilio and decide what they were going to do next. Moving woodenly and hurting all over, she returned to her office.

The moment she closed her door, her shoulders sagged and she couldn't keep tears from coming. She had been betrayed by a man she had fallen in love with and trusted.

What a little fool he must think she was.

Emilio's money may have been the only way that Brittany Beach could have been saved. But that didn't have anything to do with her heart and the deception and betrayal by Emilio. She hurt because she had given him her trust and her love and her body.

While she had been falling in love, had he and Jordan Jefferies been celebrating her naiveté and gullible acceptance?

Blind with tears, she stumbled toward the sofa to put her face in her hands and cry.

Suffering pain and anger and humiliation, she sobbed. His deception was agonizing. To know she'd been used, crushed her.

Finally, she stood and went to her bathroom to wash her face in cold water. Along with her hurt was fury over being duped, but she knew when she broke off with Emilio, what would be left after the anger had cooled would be agony.

She stared at her reflection, wanting to look composed when she saw him later tonight. Tomorrow she was taking the day off from working at Brittany Beach.

At the moment, she barely knew what she was doing.

Sitting at her desk, she switched off the lights in her office, stared outside, watching whitecaps roll in while she hurt over Emilio. She remembered the day she had asked him if something was wrong and he told her she could ask him anything she wanted. Now she could understand why he looked worried, because of guilt and the deception.

Finally, it was time to go to Emilio's condo. The sooner she broke off with him, the quicker she would begin to recover. Except, she wondered if she would ever really mend. She hoped she could control her emotions. She didn't want to shed tears around him.

She tried to concentrate on her driving, being careful because she knew she was on a rocky edge. From the lobby, she phoned to tell him she had arrived.

His voice was warm and deep. "Come up."

Stiffly, she stood in the elevator as it rose to his floor.

She stepped out in the short hallway in front of his door. He had his door open and he lounged in the doorway. Dressed in navy slacks and shirt, he leaned one broad shoulder against the doorjamb. His smile faded the moment he saw her.

"Brittany? What's wrong?" he asked, approaching her.

He walked up to place his hands on her shoulders. "What's happened?" he repeated, studying her with concern in his green eyes.

"Let's go inside," she said, knowing his hall was probably private, but she didn't want to be interrupted.

He turned to drape his arm across her shoulders as they walked into his condo and he closed the door. He turned her to face him. "What is it?"

"Parker came to see me tonight," she said. Emilio closed his eyes and rocked back on his heels.

"Brittany, let me explain," he urged. He took a deep breath, angry with himself for not confessing to her before she discovered the truth from someone else.

"My brothers have already told me about the Garrison-Jefferies feud." Her voice was cold and she stood stiffly facing him. She had lost all color, and he ached because he knew he'd hurt her.

"There's a feud, and that's why I wanted to buy into Brittany Beach," he declared earnestly. "But then, after I began to work with you, things changed and I didn't know how to tell you."

'Oh, please, Emilio! We've had enough deception between us. You used me and you got what you wanted. You've hurt my family and me. Don't add more lies and try to deceive me further. I don't want to hear any of it," she said in a tight voice as she wound her fingers together until her knuckles were white. He wanted to go wrap her in his arms and convince her that he was sincere, but he knew he couldn't. He felt as if he were sinking into quicksand that would destroy him and he knew the whole terrible situation was his own doing.

"If I'd admitted what I'd done, you would have been angry and hated me for it. If you'd learned about it from your brothers, I knew you'd be hurt and furious with me. Either way, I was doomed. To be honest, I wanted a few more nights with you when we got along well together and could make love before I told you the truth, but I was going to. I swear, I was. I knew I had to."

"Now you don't have to," she replied coldly, and her words cut into him. "For a few days you stay away from Brittany Beach."

It was over between them. There was no forgiveness in her stance and he hurt and wanted to undo what he'd done. "Brittany, listen to me," he said, approaching her to take her into his arms.

She jerked away from him. "Don't touch me! I trusted you, Emilio. You knew I believed you and you took that faith and trampled it."

"Brittany, listen to me. You're not giving me a chance here—"

"What did you give me?" she retorted and his guilt deepened. "I'll never trust you," she vowed. "We're not going to work together from here on, Emilio," she continued. "We'll arrange our schedules so that we're not at Brittany Beach at the same time."

"You're not going to listen to me at all, are you?" he asked, realizing she had shut her mind to everything he was saying.

"Get it through you head—I don't believe a word that you tell me and I don't want to see you. I'll talk to my lawyer and he can contact you and your attorney to work things out. You've taken advantage of me and deceived me and I don't want any part of you."

"I thought we had something good between us," he stated quietly.

"Coming from you, that really cuts it," she said. Her eyes flashed with fire. "You got it all from me," she said with her voice dripping with venom. "You really weren't trying to help and you weren't interested in Brittany Beach, except as a way to erode the Garrison holdings. I was a pawn in a game you were playing and you were exploiting me."

"You're not hearing one thing I'm saying to you."

"I hear you all right. I just no longer believe you," she replied.

"My feelings for you haven't changed, and I want to be with you," he said, gazing at her imploringly.

"Brittany, listen to me," he said, taking her shoulders again.

"Let me go, Emilio. I'm leaving now. I'll get someone to call you with my new schedule. When I'm at Brittany Beach, stay away. I don't want to talk to you. We've said it all right now. It's over. You got your Garrison property and you seduced me. You probably were aimed at taking one-hundred percent of Brittany Beach. That accomplishment I can keep you from doing."

"You're not being fair."

"And when were you fair?" she accused him, her brown eyes darkened with rage. "I'm out of here forever. And I guess it'll take you all of one evening before you have another adoring female draped on your arm and in your bed. By this time tomorrow, you'll forget me, except for the fact that your duplicity has been discovered and, hopefully, you can't do any further damage to the Garrisons."

"It won't be that way, and I don't want to hurt the Garrisons, particularly you," he replied.

"I hope my brothers ruin the Jefferies!"

"I don't give a damn about that," Emilio replied tersely. "It's you that I don't want to lose. I mean it, Brittany."

"We've said all there is to be said." As she headed away from him, he knew she was walking out of his life and it hurt more than he would have guessed.

Catching up with her, he walked in silence beside her and opened the elevator. When she stepped inside, she faced him.

"Don't go like this," he said.

"Goodbye, Emilio. I hope I don't see you again for a long, long time. That's the one thing you can do that will please me."

Knowing it was useless to argue with her, he stared at her, knowing he would never forget this moment. Her brown eyes were wide and still blazed with fury. Her thick brown hair was tied loosely behind her head. Her mouth was as soft and tempting as ever, but she wouldn't let him touch her again. She was beautiful, desirable and no longer part of his life.

The doors closed and she was gone. He felt as if his heart had been ripped out and taken away. As she descended to the ground floor, he watched the brass arrow above the elevator. When the arrow stopped at one, he could imagine her stepping into the lobby and walking out of his building and his life.

In a daze, he returned to his empty condo and went to the terrace to look at the traffic below, knowing she was down there, heading back to her place or Brittany Beach.

"I'm sorry I hurt you and I wish you'd listen," he said to the empty air. "I already miss you," he added, realizing he wanted her to an extent that stunned him. Had he fallen in love with her?

As he stared at the highway and tried to sort out his feelings, he frowned. He'd never been truly in love in his life. And he'd never hurt like this.

He shook his shoulders and told himself that he wasn't accustomed to women breaking off the relationship with him and he'd get over Brittany soon, the same as he had always recovered from other splits. But those other times, he had been the one to end the affair, so from the beginning he had been doing as he pleased.

Staying in his empty, silent condo was no way to get over

Brittany's loss. He picked up his billfold and keys and left to drive to El Diablo, where he could forget Brittany Garrison.

As he drove, he thought about his fifty percent of Brittany Beach. It would be a miserable partnership now for both of them. He no longer wanted to continue the feud with her family. What would he do about Jordan? He knew he couldn't convince his brother that they should call off the feud.

Getting his cell phone, Emilio contacted Jordan and got him to agree to stop by El Diablo in the morning so they could talk. Grimly, he broke the connection and headed toward his restaurant.

At half past ten, looking fresh and fit, dressed in gray slacks and a gray shirt, Jordan came striding into Emilio's office. "Morning. What's up?"

"Thanks, Jordan, for coming by," Emilio said.

"What happened to you? You look like you've been hit by a bus. What's gone wrong?"

"Have a seat."

"Something's happened, so don't keep me in suspense," Jordan said, sprawling in one of the leather chairs and placing one foot on his knee.

"Parker Garrison discovered the partnership."

"Whoo, hoo!" Jordan exclaimed with jubilation. "I hope they're burning with fury and frustration."

"They are, and so is Brittany."

Jordan's smile faded and his eyes narrowed. "So what difference does that make? Dammit, Emilio. Don't tell me you're going soft for a hot body. You can replace Brittany in five minutes."

Emilio ground his jaw closed and tried to hold his temper, knowing if they got in a fight he wouldn't get anywhere with Jordan.

"Jordan, I care about her feelings," Emilio said, walking to the window to look outside and trying to remain calm enough to reason with Jordan.

"Don't be ridiculous! She's a Garrison. You went into this wanting to take advantage of her naiveté, which you did with great success. You intended to capitalize on it and get all of Brittany Beach from her. Now, because she's letting you sleep with her—and I'm sure she is or we wouldn't be having this conversation—don't go all soft about a Garrison."

Emilio spun around, striding toward Jordan to halt only feet away. "You don't know her. She's special. She's a good businesswoman. I've got feelings for her. I'll admit that I care about her. She's different from other women."

"The hell she is!" Jordan argued, coming to his feet to glare at Emilio. "You've let her come between us. From the beginning, this is what I warned you about. You go soft on the Garrisons and she'll split us apart, Emilio. Is that what you want?"

"Of course not! You know I don't want a rift to occur. Listen to what I'm saying. We're doing fine without Brittany Beach."

"We're keeping that restaurant," Jordan insisted. "You get over her! She's not for you. From the beginning, you've lusted after her and she's probably hot in the sack, but so are other women. Get rid of her and let's go on with building our empire. We've got a great start. Don't tear us apart and wreck everything over a little hot number."

"Don't call her a 'hot number,'" Emilio ordered.

"You've let her come between us," Jordan retorted, his frown deepening while his blue eyes blazed. "You've aligned your loyalties to the Garrisons. Although I know that the Garrison men won't welcome you."

"I don't give a damn about them, and I don't want us ripped apart," Emilio replied.

"Damn straight, but we will be if you let some woman come between us."

Emilio doubled his fists and swung at Jordan, who ducked and the swing went wild without any contact. "Stop it!" Jordan shouted, stepping back out of Emilio's range and raising his fists. Locks of his blond hair curled over his forehead, while Emilio's black hair was as unruly. Emilio's chest heaved, and he fought to curb his anger.

"You're going to let her come between us, Emilio. Your loyalty should be to *us*."

"You don't have any interest in Brittany Beach, so whatever I do there, you have no control over it."

"Dammit, are you going to let her buy you out of the partnership?"

"I don't know what I'm going to do," Emilio replied bluntly.

"I'm glad our parents didn't live to see you turn traitor to the family."

"That's a hell of a thing to say!" Emilio admonished.

"If you come to your senses, give me a call," Jordan said and strode out of the room, slamming the door behind him.

Emilio's anger soared that Jordan was stubborn and unreasonable. Brittany Beach wasn't that important to them. They'd been doing fine without it, and Jordan was turning a blind eye to what Emilio wanted.

He knew Jordan disliked the Garrison men as much as he did. If Jordan would only listen and give him a chance, Emilio thought.

He swung his fist through the air in frustration and anger. He hurt over Brittany and he hated that Jordan would be unreasonable about his feelings for her. He knew his brother had a stubborn streak. Now, there was a split between them and it might widen until they couldn't bridge it.

Emilio stomped outside, standing on his patio and watching waves roll in and recede. What was he going to do about Brittany Beach?

His thoughts jumped to Brittany. He missed her. He couldn't

go an hour without thinking about her and wanting her. He cared about her and if that drove a wedge between him and his brother, so be it. Brittany was more important.

Startled that he would feel so intensely about her, he drew a deep breath. He acknowledged that she was the most important person in his life. He had known that he felt closer to her in some ways than he did to anyone else, even his brother, but he hadn't stopped to realize how vital she was to him. Why hadn't he seen this before?

Already, he missed her. He ached to go inside and phone her if for nothing else, just to hear her voice. He missed her and images of her, naked in his arms, smiling up at him, of her hands fluttering over him, of her kissing him, tormented him until he groaned and ran his fingers through his hair.

His cell phone rang and he picked up to hear his secretary telling him that Hector Garland, director of services for Brittany Beach, was in the office and wanted to see him.

"Sure, tell him to come in," Emilio said, going inside and crossing his office as the door opened and she ushered Hector inside. When Hector entered, Emilio offered his hand.

"Hi, Hector. Have a seat, please. What can I do for you?" Emilio asked as he pulled a chair around to sit and face Hector, who had a folder in his hand which he held out for Emilio.

"I brought a schedule that Brittany wanted me to give you. If you'll please follow this, the two of you will be at Brittany Beach at different times," Hector said in a brisk, businesslike voice as if he were talking about supplies they needed for the coming week.

Hurting, Emilio hoped he kept his features impassive as he accepted the folder, opened the flap and glanced at a schedule for each day of the week. "Very well. Reassure her that I'll stick to this schedule."

"Thanks," Hector replied, sounding relieved. "She asked

that anything you want, please either go through your attorney or call me or one of the other employees who can relay the message to her. She prefers that the two of you no longer have dealings with each other," he said, avoiding looking Emilio in the eye until he finished. He took a deep breath and faced Emilio. "I'm sorry."

"Thanks. So am I. Maybe with time, it'll work out," he said perfunctorily, not believing it would happen and not caring to discuss the matter with Hector. "I understand and I'll do what she wants," Emilio continued, wondering if he would keep his word on that one. He could feel the chasm between Brittany and himself widening further, getting impossible to span.

"I think that covers everything," Hector said with so much cheer, Emilio wanted to grind his teeth. "Do you have any questions or comments for me to take back to her?"

"Only what I told you a moment ago. I'll follow this schedule."

"Fine," Hector said. When he stood, Emilio came to his feet. Hector extended his hand. "As I said, I'm sorry for the split between the two of you, but this seems a workable arrangement."

"Brittany Beach has experienced, competent staff, so we'll get along," Emilio said, thinking the restaurant should thrive, but he didn't know how well he would fare in the coming weeks. Or what he would do eventually about Brittany Beach. He walked to the door with Hector and told him goodbye. The minute he closed the door behind him, he flung the folder across the office and papers spilled out on the floor.

Pacing the room, Emilio finally yanked open his office door, leaving to head to the gym and try to forget Brittany for an hour, if possible. How long before he would get over her? Like a heady wine, she was in his blood. Unlike the wine, she wasn't going to wear off any time soon.

"Dammit, Jordan!" he swore softly as he climbed into his

car. What a muddle life had become. He was paying a heavy price for deception. Was Brittany's anger enough to make her glad to be rid of him and not hurt over the end of their affair? How much had she really cared? What was she doing this moment, he wondered, wanting to be with her.

"Brittany, Brittany," he whispered while a hundred questions plagued him.

Ten

Saturday afternoon, Brittany dressed in the bedroom of a suite she had at the Garrison Grand. She had the suite so she could stay in the hotel after the rehearsal dinner and party they had last night and where today she could have a private place to change clothes.

Suspecting this wedding would be an emotional ordeal for her to get through, Brittany dressed with care, looping and pinning her hair on top of her head. A few tendrils hung down to curl slightly around her face. She smoothed the skirt of her pale yellow sleeveless silk dress and studied her reflection. While she stared at the mirror, all she could see was black wavy hair and thickly lashed green eyes. She hurt and the pain seemed to steadily increase, instead of lessen.

She resigned herself to misery and figured the time would come when the past would be a memory and the dreadful longing that enveloped her now would stop.

She suspected that she would love Emilio all her life, but she hoped she was wrong. Tears threatened and she fought them back, hating how weepy she had become when, until loving Emilio, she'd rarely shed a tear since becoming an adult.

Breaking into her thoughts, her cell phone rang. She answered to listen to Brandon, who was in the hotel for the wedding reception and wanted to know if he could talk to her privately for a few minutes. He asked her to meet him in the coffee shop, but Brittany gave him her suite number and told him to come up where they would have the most privacy.

Figuring Brandon had something that he wanted to discuss about her contract with Emilio, she walked through the suite to pick up any clothing she had discarded in the sitting area. The white carpet and white furniture looked pristine. A vase of fresh mixed flowers added to the inviting ambience and there were splashes of color in the ornate paintings on the walls and decorative pillows on the white sofa.

She carried clothes to the bedroom to hang them in the large closet. The bedroom held oak furniture and a king-size bed with a cheerful duvet of primary colors, yet neither pretty rooms and furniture or a family event could lift her sense of hurt and loss.

The knock at the door was light and she hurried to open it and smile at Brandon as she offered him her hand. Dressed in a navy suit and white shirt that complimented his tanned brown skin, he stepped inside to shake her hand.

"Stephen told me that you're here in the hotel and that you wouldn't mind if I called and wanted to talk to you."

"Of course not," she said. She motioned toward the chairs. "Please, have a seat."

As tall as Parker, Brandon moved with the energy of a well-trained athlete. He sat in a straight-backed chair and she sat on a matching one that was turned slightly toward him. "What's up, Brandon?"

"I've tried to call before but when you didn't answer, I didn't leave a message. I know Parker and Stephen—and your whole family now—have learned about your partnership with Emilio Jefferies."

"Yes. Parker and Stephen finally calmed down."

"I wanted to talk to you myself. When you first called me about the partnership, you know I couldn't warn you further than I tried to, because of my attorney-client relationship with Parker and Stephen."

"I understand, and Parker and I discussed your position. I know you couldn't reveal their situation with Emilio and his brother. I told Parker that you tried to discourage me from entering into the partnership. I didn't guess the real reason for your remarks."

"That's the most I could say, but I felt terrible, Brittany, because I knew you were going into something that would enrage your entire family. Parker and Stephen were wild about it because they fight Emilio and Jordan constantly."

"I must have been the only person in SoBe who was ignorant of the feud," she said bitterly, and then remembered Brandon and tried to smile at him. "Sorry, Brandon. None of it was your fault at all, and don't worry about it. I understand, and you did your ethical best to keep me from it."

"Thanks for being understanding about this, because I know it's caused you pain. If I can do anything to help you in any way—"

She shook her head. "Forget it, but thanks," she said, interrupting him. "It was one of life's lessons, both for me and my brothers, who in the future may not keep me in the dark about business matters."

"Well, I hate that it happened." Brandon stood. "I'll go now. It'll soon be time for Parker's wedding."

"I really meant what I said. Don't worry about telling me

about the Jefferies, because I know you did all you could," she said, standing when he did. "It was particularly kind of you to come by to talk to me about it."

"It's damn little when you consider what happened," he said. "I'll see you shortly," he added.

Smiling at him, she hoped that she had convinced him that she held him in no blame, whatsoever. When he left, she closed the door and leaned against it. What would she have done if he'd told her about the feud? She'd had nowhere else to turn. Yet she knew she wouldn't have entered into the contract with Emilio. How could he have been so duplicitous with her?

Before going downstairs, she went back to the bedroom to look one more time at herself. Knowing she had to get through this wedding without losing control of her emotions, she reminded herself again that today belonged to Parker and Anna and she didn't want to darken it in the slightest. "No tears for the next five hours," she said aloud to her image in the mirror.

"Damn you, Emilio!" she snapped, wondering if he and Jordan were still celebrating the wreckage they had caused in the Garrison family.

Taking a deep breath, she really looked at herself and decided her appearance was fine. She had lost a slight bit of weight, but nothing noticeable yet.

When Parker returned to work after his wedding, she wanted to talk to him about taking the land where Brittany Beach was located. If they were evicted and had to find another location, she figured Emilio would want out of the partnership. She knew that Parker would help her buy Emilio out in a flash.

On the other hand, if Jordan and Emilio were set on ruining the Garrison empire, they might hang on, just to have part of the Garrison property. If so, she wanted to sell her half and find some other job and, again, her brothers would help do anything, she suspected, to get her out of business with Emilio.

She left her suite to go to her brother's wedding.

They had a private area on the beach where chairs had been set up. The sunny afternoon was perfect, with only a faint breeze, whitecaps washing ashore and receding. The deep-aqua water met a blue sky. A band was to one side of sprays of red and white roses.

Brittany slid into a seat by Brooke, who looked unusually glum. Studying her twin, Brittany knew distance had grown between them, yet there was still a bond that would always be there.

"Are you all right?" she asked Brooke, who turned to look into her eyes. Brittany's suspicion strengthened that something worried Brooke, but Brooke merely nodded and smiled.

"I'm fine. What about you? Adam told me about Emilio Jefferies. Sorry, Brit."

Nodding, Brittany bit her lip. "Thanks. I didn't know anything about our feud with the Jefferies, but I'm sure you did," she whispered, unable to curb a surge of anger over her family's attitude toward her.

"Yes, I did and I figured you did, too," Brooke said. "Otherwise, I would've told you. Here comes Adam to seat Anna's mother," she said and Brittany glanced around at an attractive woman on her youngest brother's arm.

"Look at Stephen," Brooke hissed. "He's going to seat Mom and he looks unhappy."

Brittany glanced around to see Bonita walking beside Stephen. Her mother's step was steady and she had a faint smile. She looked more like her old self, in a beautiful pale blue silk dress. Brittany knew from talking to her that Bonita had been drinking since morning, yet she was hiding it well so far.

The minister appeared, striding to the front, followed by

Parker in a charcoal suit. Parker's gaze went to the back where Brittany guessed Anna waited for her entrance cue. Parker looked happier than ever.

Something twisted deep inside and she clenched her fists and fought thinking about people in love.

Then the wedding march began and everyone stood and turned to watch the bride.

Eleven

On the arm of her father, Anna looked radiant in a short, white silk sleeveless dress with a low-cut *V* neckline. She wore a spray of white flowers in her hair with a veil that was turned back. Her sparkling green eyes were locked on Parker. A pang stabbed Brittany as a different a pair of thickly lashed green eyes taunted her memory, and moments in Emilio's arms swept her thoughts, far from Parker's wedding. How she ached for Emilio.

She tried to concentrate on Parker and Anna repeating their vows, but all she could think about was Emilio. She glanced at her watch several times until Brooke turned to give her a searching look.

When the ceremony was over and the party started, Brittany was relieved. The band's lively music played. Tables had been set up and white-coated waiters formally dressed—except for their sandals—moved through the crowd. A buffet was spread on three long tables with an array of appealing dishes, but

Brittany had no appetite and she simply carried a wineglass so no one would bother her about a drink, but she didn't want that, either.

Brittany was happy for Parker and Anna, but she hurt and she wanted to be away from the crowd and home, where she could be alone with her pain. Knowing that she had a room in the hotel and soon could escape to solitude, she forced herself to move through the crowd and welcome guests. She didn't feel like partying, and it was an effort to try to keep a smile on her face and remain friendly.

She congratulated Anna, giving her a hug. "Welcome to the family. You're officially my sister now."

"Thanks, Brittany," Anna replied with a big smile. "That's kind and I hope we truly are."

"You look gorgeous."

"Thank you," Anna repeated, and then Brittany turned to hug Parker.

"Congratulations, Big Brother. I didn't think this day would ever happen. I wish you and Anna all the best."

"Thanks, Brittany. I appreciate it and I can't quite believe this day is here, myself," Parker said amiably and grinned, turning to look at his bride. Brittany wondered if he was even conscious of the crowd, family or friends. She laughed, patting his shoulder as Adam appeared.

"Congratulations, brother. May you be married a hundred years," Adam said and turned to Anna. "Anna, Brittany, Parker, this is Heidi Summers," Adam said, introducing a tall, stunning blonde whom everyone greeted perfunctorily.

The kind of beautiful woman that Emilio might like, Brittany thought bitterly, recalling pictures of Emilio with models and rising starlets.

She didn't wait to hear Parker's reply, but left with a softly mumbled, "Excuse me, I'll speak to Mother," she said.

She spotted Bonita, who was seated at a table with Brooke beside her. Brittany squared her shoulders and walked over to talk to them. She should sit and relieve Brooke, who would probably like to escape Bonita's sharp criticisms, but Brittany didn't care to compound her glum feelings by sitting with her mother.

In spite of her increased alcohol dependency, Bonita continued to be stylish, which surprised Brittany, yet she suspected they could all thank Lisette, hairdressers and some clerks in exclusive shops who sent clothes out for Bonita's approval. Always thin, she had lost weight and become even more fragile-looking since her husband's death.

Vowing she wouldn't stay more than another ten minutes with her mother, Brittany did her dutiful daughter act and walked over to sit across from Brooke and their mother.

"Hi, Mother. Beautiful wedding, wasn't it?"

"I don't know why she couldn't have the formal church wedding that Parker deserved," Bonita replied sharply. "The beach is dreadful with all this sand everywhere." Bonita's words were clipped as she studied Brittany. "I heard about you taking in an enemy of the family as your partner. How could you do that?"

"I've been over this with Parker. I didn't know Emilio was a Garrison enemy. No one told me about the Garrisons and the Jefferies," she replied stiffly, realizing even their mother had known about the feud. When they kept her in the dark about everything, what did the family expect?

She tuned Bonita out and, in seconds, stood and moved away, feeling chilled and clammy in spite of the warm August afternoon. It was almost September. Time would help, she reminded herself.

Adam approached her, carrying two drinks. Wind tangled locks of his black hair.

"You beat a hasty retreat," he said, looking at her with curiosity.

She shrugged. "I talked to Mom, who's more critical than

ever and probably had too much to drink by ten o'clock this morning."

"I know," Adam answered grimly, his blue eyes clouding with worry. "I haven't introduced Heidi yet, and I don't know that I will, although our mother is hiding her liquor well, so far."

"She's had plenty of practice. And it won't matter whether you introduce your friend or not. Mom won't like her. Adam, when are you going to get rid of the bimbos and settle down?" she asked her tall brother. "You're thirty."

"I love beautiful women," he answered with an infectious grin. "Sis, it ain't gonna happen," he joked. "If I want someone with a brain, I can go talk to Parker and Stephen. That's not why I'm with Heidi," he said and moved on as she shook her head.

"Womanizer," Brittany said softly under her breath, always surprised that Adam had a way with women, because as far as the family was concerned, he was a loner. Often excusing him for it, Brittany knew that he was younger than Parker and Stephen by quite a few years, while she and Brooke had grown up doing things that wouldn't interest a boy. He was a notorious playboy and she wondered how old they would all be when, and if, Adam ever settled.

As she wandered through the crowd, speaking to first one guest and then another, she saw an unmistakable tall, pretty redheaded woman dressed in a sleeveless green sheath. She stood talking to Anna. Brittany knew Megan Simmons and strolled to the two women to say hello.

"Megan," Brittany said, "I heard you were back in town, and I'm glad you're here."

Turning, Megan smiled. "Hi, Brittany. Thanks. I'm a resident again. I was talking to Anna, who's a beautiful bride."

"Yes, she is," Brittany agreed, smiling at Anna. "We're fortunate to have her in our family and she's turned my all-business brother into a human being."

Megan smiled while Anna laughed. "Thanks, you two," Anna said. When she glanced across the crowd, Brittany knew she was looking at Parker. Suspecting Anna was barely listening to any conversation even when she was involved in it, Brittany looked at Megan.

"I heard that you're a partner in your former design firm now. Congratulations!"

"Thanks," she replied. "I'm getting settled in and started. This is a great place to be an interior designer. I love the art deco that makes SoBe unique."

"Come to my restaurant, Brittany Beach, sometime soon. If you'll let me know, I'll buy your dinner."

"Thanks, Brittany," Megan said, smiling at her. "That's a nice offer and I'll take you up on it," she said, but something in her voice made Brittany suspect that Megan was merely being polite in her reply.

"Here comes my brother," Brittany said, seeing Stephen with a somber expression as he strode toward them. He had shed the coat to his navy suit. Wind caught locks of his jet-black hair and he moved with that same athletic ease that Emilio did.

"It was really nice to see you, Brittany," Megan said hastily. "Best wishes to you, Anna, and to Parker. If you both will excuse me, I see someone," Megan added and turned to hurry away, disappearing into the crowd of milling guests.

"What was all that about?" Brittany said, looking at Anna, who shrugged.

"She seemed to be enjoying everything until seconds ago," Anna remarked. "I guess she saw an old friend."

"Here's Stephen," Brittany said, watching her brother stride up to them.

"That was Megan Simmons, wasn't it?" he said as if to himself. "How come she left so quickly?"

"I don't know," Anna answered. "She said something about seeing someone."

"Stephen, did you hire her to do the Garrison Grand?" Brittany asked. "I think she's really good at what she does."

His gaze searched the crowd and, for a moment, Brittany wondered if he had even heard her question.

"I've called her several times to talk to her about the hotel, but she won't return my calls," he said.

"Did you leave a message?" Brittany asked.

"Yes, I did. I'll get in touch with her," he said and Brittany noticed a muscle worked in his jaw. "Excuse me, you two," he said and left them, turning his head to look at the guests.

"Well, what was all that about?" Brittany asked.

"I don't know. I can't imagine why she isn't returning Stephen's calls. Maybe Parker should call her."

Brittany laughed. "Stephen will not get his big brother to call her for him!"

At that moment, she saw Adam and Heidi approaching. "I'm leaving you to Adam and his latest woman, who will probably be replaced tomorrow," Brittany remarked drily and moved on, looking to see who else she'd missed talking to. She saw Brandon in a cluster of men with Parker. He glanced her way, nodded and smiled and she waved her hand in return.

"Brittany," Brooke called and Brittany turned to find Brooke approaching her.

"So you escaped from Mom's side," Brittany said.

"Yes. Some old-time friends are with her and Lisette is hovering in the background, so I left."

"Adam's good about watching her on Sunday evenings, but he won't want to now with a hot blonde hanging on his arm."

"Stephen has his yacht, Adam has his women," Brooke said. "I think Parker has his concerns. Anna is a big influence on him."

"An astounding influence," Brittany agreed and heard a commotion.

"Oh, saints in heaven!" Brittany exclaimed, stiffening, and Brooke reached out to grab her arm.

"Brittany, what's wrong? Are you all right? You look as if you've seen a ghost. What's the racket?" Brooke asked and Brittany broke free to start running.

Twelve

To Brittany's horror, Emilio had crashed Parker's wedding!

For an instant, her heart stopped and she forgot everything except him. He was in a conservative charcoal suit and, in spite of his angry expression, looked incredibly handsome. Then her heart-pounding second of shock was gone.

Emilio shouted at Stephen and Adam, while the brothers, including Parker, yelled at Emilio, whose jaw was set in a stubborn line. Brittany's heart pounded. There could be only one reason for Emilio to crash Parker's wedding.

"No! Get out!" she yelled, knowing her cries were lost in all the shouting.

Adam and Stephen restrained Parker, who was ready to fight Emilio.

Brandon took Emilio's arm, but Emilio pushed him away and charged ahead, searching the crowd and then looking at her.

Before he could get to Brittany, Bonita stepped in front of

him, and he stopped in his tracks. Everyone froze, as Bonita waved her fist at Emilio.

"You bastard!" she snarled. "You're a deceitful outsider who tried to steal what wasn't yours," she continued. "You've never belonged in society, anyway!"

"Oh, my heavens!" Brooke exclaimed. "We've got to get Mom," she said as she rushed forward.

Bonita continued to insult Emilio, who had made it past all the Garrison men, only to be halted by their mother.

Adam and Brooke rushed to Bonita and each took her arm and walked her away from Emilio.

Brittany knew they needed to get Bonita away from the guests. Alcohol had taken its toll on her. Then Brittany forgot about Bonita as she watched Emilio, who rushed toward her while stunned guests stood as if captured in a picture.

"Get out of here," Brittany said in a low voice. "You've caused enough trouble."

"I have to talk to you and I'm not leaving until I do," Emilio informed her. She saw the steely look in his eyes and knew he meant what he said. Her pulse roared in her ears and she wished she could faint and be oblivious to everything.

Instead, she jerked her head and put her hand on his arm. "Come with me. Hurry!" she said, glancing beyond him to see Stephen and Parker starting toward them.

She rushed with Emilio into the hotel, praying they didn't encounter her mother inside.

It seemed an eternity to cross the lobby and get an elevator, but finally doors closed on them and they were alone. She was breathing as hard as if she had run a race as she looked at him.

"I want to talk to you and I want you to listen to me," he said.

"You picked a poor way to do this."

"You won't take my calls. You won't come to the restaurant if I'm there and you leave if I arrive unannounced."

"Indeed, I do," she said, raising her chin in defiance, ignoring her racing pulse or the ache caused by seeing him. "You know I don't want to be with you, or even talk to you and this is a strain right now. Besides that, you've interrupted the wedding reception and created bad moments that Anna and Parker will remember the rest of their lives."

"For that, I'm profoundly sorry, but this is the only way I could get to you. I'll apologize to your entire family and try to make it up in some manner to Parker and his bride. I had to see you. I want to talk to you, and you've put me off long enough."

She rode in silence until they reached her floor. She unlocked the door to her suite and they stepped inside. As soon as they did, Emilio closed and locked the door while she dropped the key onto a table.

When she turned to face him, he withdrew a thick sheaf of folded papers from his inside coat pocket. "This is for you. I want you to read it over and decide what you want to do," he said solemnly.

Surprised and puzzled, she took the paper from him and unfolded it to see that she was holding a contract. "What's this?" she asked, glancing at him.

"It makes you sole owner of Brittany Beach once again. You can buy back my part and, because of the anguish I caused you, I'll sell it to you for a million and a half. Brittany Beach will belong solely to you."

Stunned, she scanned the contract and saw it was exactly what he'd told her. "You'd do this?"

"Yes, to try to make things right for you."

"Does Jordan know about this?"

"Not yet, but he will," Emilio replied calmly, his gaze going slowly over her features as if he were trying to memorize them.

"Doesn't he have to agree to this?" she asked.

"No. I can do what I want. You buy it back and the money will go into our business account."

"He won't like it, will he?" she persisted, amazed at what Emilio was doing.

"No, but returning what I took from you is more important. Your feelings come first with me."

Shocked, she looked again at the contract. She could buy him out and her restaurant could be hers once again, solely a Garrison endeavor. "What happened to this big feud between our two families?" she asked.

He shrugged. "I want no part of it. Jordan hasn't changed, so he's determined to build a Jefferies empire to rival the Garrisons and he'll clash with your brothers."

"He'll be so angry with you," she said, staring at Emilio and thinking about what his offer really meant to her. "He'll be even angrier if you don't get back your full two million. How can you do this if it drives a wedge between you and your brother?"

"It's necessary. I don't want to fight any Garrison, one woman in particular. I hope Jordan will come around. Whether he does or not shouldn't matter to you. I know you and your family would like to buy back my partnership. Is Brandon here? He told me he was coming."

"Yes, he is," she said, barely able to get out the words.

"I've already signed the contract. Turn to the last pages and you'll see my signature. If we add yours in front of a notary, it's a done deal and you will once again be sole owner of Brittany Beach. You'll have your restaurant back and you can go on packing them in and running Brittany Beach and your brothers will leave you alone to do so."

Shaken, she stared at him. "I'm overwhelmed and don't know what to say."

He took the few steps necessary to close the distance between them. Reaching out, he folded her cold fingers in his warm, strong hands. His intense regard made her pulse hum and, in spite of all that had happened, she wanted him and wanted his arms around her.

"I miss you more than I thought possible," he said in a rasping voice that made her tremble. "I love you, Brittany."

Her surprise deepened even more, and she looked at him while her heart accelerated.

"Our families hate each other," she whispered, thinking how angry her brothers had been at Emilio.

"I can't do anything about families, mine or yours. I just know what I want and it's you. I don't want to go through my life without you in it. I love you. I want you to marry me."

Another shock jolted her. While Emilio's words echoed in her thoughts, she felt consumed by the pure green of his eyes that bored into her. Their families might not ever like each other—was she ready to live with that? She couldn't answer her own question, but she did know that she loved Emilio. She took a deep breath and stepped closer to wrap her arms around his neck.

"I love you," she whispered, standing on tiptoe to kiss him.

His strong arms banded her and drew her into his tight embrace as he leaned over her to kiss her passionately. His deep, long kiss conveyed all his feelings for her.

Her heart thudded and she wound her fingers in his hair and knew Emilio's love was what she wanted more than anything else. She tipped back to look at him, framing his face with her hands. "It's been terrible to be away from you," she whispered. "I love you and, yes, I'll marry you."

His eyes blazed with desire and he dipped his head again to kiss her hard. Suddenly, she didn't want the barriers between them. Her hands flew over him as swiftly as his fluttered over her. She twisted free buttons and slid down his zipper and in minutes, clothes were discarded as they kissed. He picked her up into his arms to carry her to the bedroom.

Emilio yanked away the linens on the bed and placed her on it, kneeling to kiss her throat and then trail kisses lower to her breast. She moaned and sat up to wrap her arms around him while he bent over her and his mouth covered hers as he kissed her passionately.

She felt starved for him, and ran her hand over his warm, muscled shoulder as she kissed him.

He shifted, showering kisses lower to her breasts, taking her nipple in his mouth to circle the tip with his tongue. His hand drifted across her belly and between her thighs.

He stopped, walking away to retrieve a condom from the pocket of his pants and then returned and moved between her legs.

Her heart raced with eagerness. She reached for him, wanting to pull him to her, aching for him while she watched him put on the latex shield. She ran her hands along his muscled thighs and then he lowered himself to thrust into her.

Wrapping her legs around him and her arms around his neck, she held him tightly as her hips arched against him and she moved frantically with him. How starved she was for him! "Emilio, I love you!" she cried.

Wanting him more than ever, she rocked with him, the tension building to white heat. Finally, she shook with release while she felt him shudder with his climax.

Ecstasy replaced need as her breathing slowed and she relaxed in his embrace. Taking her with him, he rolled on his side and held her close to kiss her with satisfaction. "I have to hear you say it again," he whispered and leaned back a fraction to look at her as he stroked her hair away from her face. "I love you. Will you marry me?"

"Yes, I'll marry you."

He looked at her solemnly. "We both have families that won't approve. You may face a real battle with them and I know I will with Jordan. Are you ready to live with their anger?" He placed his finger on her lips. "Think about it before you answer me."

She wound her fingers in his damp chest hair and ran her hand over his hip while she imagined how furious each member of her family would be. Bonita would be in a rage. So would Parker and Stephen. Brooke and Adam—they might accept it. Emilio shifted his hand away to toy with long locks of her hair.

"I'm not giving up the man I love to keep my family happy," she replied and saw some of the tenseness go out of his expression, even though he still watched her thoughtfully.

"It won't be easy. I can promise you that."

"Since you'll let me buy back your partnership at a bargain price, none of them will be as angry as they were, except my mother. Right now, she's furious over other things. She's got problems, Emilio."

"Jordan will still compete with them and annoy them, so don't hope for peace," Emilio said. "The feud will continue. Make no mistake about it, Brittany."

"I know you're right," she answered soberly. "But I'm sure about what I want to do." Suddenly, she flashed a broad smile. "Oh, yes, I'll marry you," she repeated with joy, pulling his head down to kiss him a long time.

Wrapping his arms tightly around her, he kissed her in return.

Finally, when she leaned away, she studied him. "Are you sure about what you're doing? You're not exactly the marrying type."

"That's because you hadn't come into my life."

She smiled and hugged him.

"I never want to go through days without you—and nights. Especially the nights. I couldn't sleep or eat or work. I love you and I want you with me and I want to marry you," Emilio repeated.

She kissed him again and finally snuggled against him. "I love you," she whispered. "I can't say it enough."

"I can't hear it enough," he answered. "When we marry, perhaps we can run our two businesses together. We were doing a good job the short time we worked together."

She raised up slightly to prop her head on her hand and study him. "You'll let me run El Diablo with you?"

"I'll give you El Diablo if I have to, just to get you to marry me. Of course, I will. You're doing a great job with Brittany Beach and your family, including Parker, acknowledged that until I got involved in it."

"They still don't know about the embezzlement."

"That's history and they don't need to know. What about running our businesses together?"

"I think it sounds like a great idea," she replied, smiling at him and running her index finger along his smooth jaw.

"Brittany, I interrupted Parker and Anna's wedding, which I'll apologize for and send them some kind of gift to make up for the disturbance. I think in the interest of smoothing things over now, you should go back to the reception for a time while I'll slip quietly away."

"You're probably right," she said with a sigh, hating to part.

"When you leave here, I want you to call me and meet me at my condo."

"Family events take time," she replied, winding a short lock of his hair around her finger as she leaned over him. "I think I should wait until tomorrow at Sunday dinner to announce our engagement, because I don't want to do so right now. This is Parker's and Anna's time and all the attention should be on them.

"Later, I'll call Parker and leave a message on his cell phone about our engagement. Parker won't care what happens for a time because he's so in love with Anna that he's in a daze."

"When you go downstairs, take the contract and show it to

Parker and the others. Brittany Beach will revert to the Garrisons."

"Your cooperation will go a long way toward smoothing things over with my family. Maybe you can drop by after dinner tomorrow so you can meet the ones you don't know and get reacquainted with Stephen and Adam on a better basis. Parker and Anna won't be there because they'll be on their honeymoon."

"If they don't want me, don't push it," Emilio said as he sat up. "I don't want to, but I'll shower and get out of here."

She slipped her arms around his neck to pull his head down and kiss him while her heart raced with joy and eagerness. Finally, she released him and watched him cross the room. He was nude, fit, virile and she wanted to call him back to bed, but she knew they had to wait.

It was thirty minutes later when she stepped outside, paused and searched the crowd still enjoying the reception. The moment she spotted Parker, she hurried to him and tugged on his arm.

Standing in a crowd of guests, Parker laughed at something someone said. He glanced at her and his smile faded. Excusing himself, he turned to walk away with her.

"I want to talk to you. Emilio gave me this," she said. She held out the contract. He glanced at it and her and then took it from her and scanned the first page. His head came up and she could see the surprise on his face, which for Parker was unusual.

"He let us buy him out? And for less money? What strings are there?"

"It's signed. No strings. As soon as I sign it and have it notarized, Brittany Beach is mine, plus half a million that he put into the business."

"I'll be damned." Parker's eyes narrowed. "No one does this unless there's a reason."

"There is a reason, Parker," she declared flatly, wondering

how her family would take her relationship with Emilio. "Emilio and I love each other."

"I'll be damned," Parker said again, staring at her intently. "Emilio Jefferies? You're sure, aren't you?"

"Yes, I am."

"He damn well must love you to do this. His brother may never speak to him again," Parker said, looking at the last page and Emilio's signature. "You'll alienate yourself from your family, as well," Parker said sharply.

"That won't be anything new," she said, his words cutting into her. "Go on and enjoy your wedding party. I'll let Stephen and the rest of the family know about this contract and Brittany Beach."

"I'm shocked," Parker admitted. "It isn't often I get surprised by someone, but this is twice Emilio's surprised me."

"Go on, Parker. Enjoy your day," she said, giving him a small push. He smiled and walked away and she suspected he was already thinking about his bride again. She glanced around for Stephen, to show him the contract.

It was nine o'clock that night when she walked into Emilio's condo and into his arms.

She felt even more urgency to kiss and love him than she had earlier in the afternoon and he seemed to share the feeling.

Later, when they calmed and he held her close against his warm, naked body, she ran her hand across his chest. "I couldn't wait to see you," she said.

"I couldn't wait for you to get here." He shifted to look at her. "There's something I've been thinking about. How much did you search for your accountant?"

"I hired a private detective who worked about two weeks and said the man was no longer in Miami. He could have gone anywhere in the world, so I gave up. Why?" she asked, toying with a lock of Emilio's black hair.

"I'd like to hire a P.I. to hunt for him. Let the P.I. take some time and have enough funds to do a thorough job. We might be able to find the guy and get your money."

"I don't think you'll find him."

"Do you have any objections if I give it a try?"

"No, I don't, but I think you're wasting your money."

"I might be, but I want someone to try to track the guy."

She twisted to kiss Emilio lightly and then she smiled at him. "Go ahead and hunt for him."

"I love you," he said, gazing into her eyes. "I want you in my arms every night. Just a minute," he said, extricating himself and slipping off the bed. She watched him in the dim light of the bedroom as he left the room and returned.

He slid back in bed beside her, pulling them both up on pillows and holding her close against him. "I have something for you," he said. "Hold out your hand."

"What on earth?" she said, looking at him. "You can't have it in a pocket and I don't see that you have anything in your hands." Then she noticed one fist was closed and she looked at him questioningly.

He held out his hand. "This is for you." He opened his hand and she gasped. A huge diamond sparkled in the soft light. The seven-carat diamond was on a gold band, surrounded by rows of smaller diamonds.

"Emilio! It's beautiful!" she cried.

"Hold out your hand," he commanded and, when she did, he slipped it on her finger. It was heavy, the thick gold shiny, the diamonds dazzling and she turned her hand first one way and then another.

"It's magnificent!" She looked at him and then threw her arms around his neck to kiss him and push him down in the bed and, within minutes, she forgot about her ring and was lost in making love with him.

Sunday, she stayed at his condo until mid-afternoon, when she suddenly sat up in bed. "I want to get home early to talk to my mother and tell her about our engagement before telling the others."

"That's the right thing to do. I should go see her and see Parker, to tell them that I want to marry you. If your oldest brother hadn't just married, I would have waited to ask you until I told him."

"Thank goodness you didn't! Don't be old-fashioned about this."

"I intended to be quite old-fashioned about it, but I've blown it a little by proposing first."

"I want to call her and tell her I'm coming early," Brittany said and climbed out of bed.

Later, as she finished combing her hair under Emilio's watchful gaze, she glanced in the mirror at him. "How do I look?"

"The only way you could look better," he said, letting his eyes drift slowly over her pink shirt and gray slacks, "would be naked."

"Why did I even ask," she said, and took one more look in the mirror before facing him. "If everyone is receptive to my announcement that we're engaged, I'd like you to come to the house tonight. Can I call you?"

He looked amused. "Want me to drive to Bal Harbour and eat somewhere nearby so I'll be on hand?"

"Would you?" she asked in surprise. She was excited and eager to get their engagement into the open for the world to know.

"I don't mind," he said easily, amusement dancing in his green eyes. "I'll have my cell phone. Give me a call."

"Sweet!" she exclaimed. "You're wonderful!"

He caught her around the waist to kiss her long and hard until she pushed away. "I have to go," she said, twisting free and hurrying to get her purse and car keys and kiss him goodbye once more at the elevator door.

Excitement bubbled in her and even the prospect of her mother still being angry over Emilio's appearance yesterday couldn't dampen her happiness.

Dressed in flawless white silk slacks and a matching blouse, Bonita waited alone on the veranda, the ever-present drink in her hand.

Brittany kissed her mother's cheek and sat beside her. "I wanted to talk to you before the others come. Stephen said he was going to tell you that Emilio offered to sell me back my ownership of Brittany Beach. It'll be half a million dollars less than he paid."

"He should do that. It was awful of him to take advantage of you," Bonita said and sipped her drink.

"He's made up for it. Mother, he's asked me to marry him, and I wanted to tell you first. He said he wanted to come meet you and tell you."

Bonita focused on her daughter and Brittany remembered better times with her mother. Brittany reached over to pat her mother's hand. "I love him."

"Don't let him break your heart. I've seen his pictures in the paper," Bonita said. "He likes women."

"He loves me and I love him very much."

"Don't rush into this, Brittany. His family feuds with our family. You'll go into a marriage that has obstacles before it even starts. That kind of man isn't faithful. Your marriage won't last."

"Yes, it will," she said, disappointed and sitting back in her chair. "We love each other and we plan to marry," she said firmly.

"Have you set a date?"

"No, we haven't."

"Think about it and give it time. Men like that—he's not going to be a good husband."

"I think we'll love each other all our lives. We like to be together. We like some of the same things. We work well together. That's more than a lot of couples have."

"You have no idea what the future will bring. A man like that, wealth and looks and a playboy, he can't be trusted," Bonita said, frowning.

"I think he can and I love him. Sometime tonight, I want to tell the rest of the family. After dinner, I'd like to ask him to come by to meet you and Brooke. He knows the men in the family."

Nodding, Bonita took a long drink. "Men are rotten," she said quietly and Brittany suspected Bonita had already dismissed her and her announcement from her mind.

Brittany heard Stephen talking to Lisette and she stood to greet him. "Here comes Stephen," she said, relieved to have the moment with Bonita over as she turned to see Stephen stride onto the veranda.

Dressed in a tan sport shirt and chinos, he look fit and happy as he greeted her. Soon, the family was all together, seated in a circle. Brittany was surprised how pleasant the atmosphere was. Brooke, who was in blue slacks and a blue-and-white silk shirt, sipped a glass of water.

Stephen gave Brittany a long, searching look. "Here's a toast to Brittany. Here's to sis for having her restaurant and a tidy chunk of money back in her sole ownership," he said, surprising her.

"I'll be happy to toast that," she said, as she raised her glass and the others did at the same time. They lightly touched glasses.

"I'm glad that's made the family so happy," she said, smiling at them, thinking nothing could mar her joy this night.

"So do you plan any changes as soon as you're back as sole owner?" Stephen asked and she shook her head.

"No. Nothing really changed, anyway. It wasn't a long time that Emilio was involved."

"No, it wasn't. By the way, all of you, next week I'm having a casual party on my yacht. Everyone's invited. It's a bunch of friends, but family is always welcome," Stephen announced and conversation shifted from her restaurant.

Brittany could hardly concentrate on the conversation that swirled around her on the veranda or later at dinner. Eagerness simmered in her and she waited, trying to decide if this was the night to break the news of her engagement or if she should wait.

Her siblings seemed in good moods and, for once, there wasn't much tension at the table. Dimly, she wondered if Parker's absence on his honeymoon contributed to a more relaxed atmosphere, but she decided that wasn't the difference. Finally, she couldn't wait any longer.

"I have an announcement," she said and everyone except Bonita looked expectantly at her.

"If it tops the one you had yesterday," Stephen remarked lightly, "let's hear it."

"You might not think so, but I think it does." She fished in her pocket and slipped her ring on her finger beneath the table and then raised her hand. Adam was the first to notice.

"Uh-oh," he said. "I see diamonds," Adam said, grinning. "What a ring!"

"Emilio asked me to marry him and we're engaged," she said, smiling broadly. "I've already told Mother."

"Brittany!" Brooke exclaimed, her eyes widening. "You and Emilio?"

"You're marrying a Jefferies," Stephen said evenly and she wondered if he hated the thought. She looked at him and smiled, but he didn't return her smile.

"I've warned her against marrying a Jefferies," Bonita said glumly.

Everyone started talking at once and Brittany answered their questions and finally waved her hand at them. "I want to call Emilio. He came to Bal Harbour because I asked him to and I want him to come to the house and get acquainted," she said, looking directly at Stephen, who would be the most likely to object.

"I think that's a good idea," Stephen said, stepping into the void left by Parker as a family spokesperson.

As soon as they finished dinner, she rushed from the table to call him. Next, she went to the kitchen, where she found Lisette and told her the news, which was received with all the warmth Brittany had hoped her mother would show.

Half an hour later, the family was on the veranda when Brittany's phone vibrated and she left the family to take the call. Emilio said he was at the front door, so she hurried to greet him. The minute she opened the door, she stood on tiptoe to kiss him.

He was in navy slacks and a navy sport shirt and he looked handsome.

"How'd they take the news of the engagement?" he asked.

"Fine," she said, hoping he didn't ask in particular about her mother. "They'll be friendly. You'll see. And come with me real quickly to the kitchen to meet Lisette."

She took his hand and as soon as he had met and talked a few minutes to Lisette, they walked through the house to the veranda, where the men came to their feet as she introduced Emilio to Bonita and Brooke. He already knew Stephen and Adam, who shook hands with him.

To her relief, everyone greeted him with a friendly smile; even Bonita rose to the occasion and was the gracious hostess for a few minutes before lapsing into silence.

"Welcome to the family," Brooke said, smiling at him as if

there had never been a problem and Brittany had a rush of gratitude for her sister.

"Thank you, I feel very fortunate," Emilio said, draping his arm lightly across Brittany's shoulders.

"Have a seat," Stephen urged. "You're the man of the hour, anyway, for your magnanimous gesture, letting her buy out your ownership in Brittany Beach. How could we not welcome you after that?" he asked, and she wondered if there was a ripple of tension between Stephen and Emilio, but they both smiled and she relaxed.

Her relief increased when Emilio seemed to fit into the group and was his usual charming self. Once her worries about the announcement and how he would be received were over, she simply wanted to be alone with him.

He showed interest in Stephen's yacht and, in a short time, she was surprised to listen to Stephen inviting Emilio to come with Brittany to his party.

By ten o'clock, Emilio stood. "I've enjoyed this, but it's time I should get back to South Beach. Thanks for the fine welcome you've given me," he said.

Brittany stood and when they had all said goodbyes, she walked to the front with Emilio and stepped outside with him to stand on tiptoe and kiss him lightly.

He slipped his arm around her waist and held her close. "Come to my condo from here, will you?"

"Yes. They liked you. Stephen liked you enough to invite you onboard his yacht."

"Your oldest brother may be the tough one to win over. We've had some royal battles over property and deals."

"We're not going to worry about Parker now," she said and he smiled at her.

"I love you," he said softly and leaned over to kiss her. In minutes, she pushed against him.

"I'll see you before long," she said and watched him get in his car and drive away.

Humming, she joined her family. "Thank all of you for being yourselves and nice and welcoming him," she said.

"He's acquiring a family," Adam said.

"And he may be losing a brother," Stephen added drily and Brittany wondered if he was right. She sat and talked to her family for the next half hour and then they all told Bonita good night.

As Brittany was getting into her car, Brooke hurried out. "Brittany, wait," she called and joined her sister. "Congratulations again and I'm happy for both of you."

"Thanks and, again, thanks for being so nice tonight. That could have been awkward, but it wasn't."

"I know. I'm glad."

Brittany impulsively hugged Brooke. "Thanks again. You take care of yourself."

"Sure," Brooke replied seriously and stepped back, while Brittany climbed into her car. Brooke turned to go to her own car.

It seemed an eternity until Brittany finally entered Emilio's condo. Smiling at her, he drew her into his embrace. "I couldn't wait to be alone with you!" he whispered, leaning down to kiss her.

Ecstatic to be engaged and to be in his arms and have had her family accept him, Brittany kissed him. Finally, she leaned back and looked up at him. "I love you," she whispered.

"You're my life, my love. I know I have to be the most fortunate man on earth."

Joy welled in each of them and spilled over into huge smiles. They could hardly take their eyes from each other, wanting to memorize this moment. She knew she was fortunate that she was held tightly in the embrace of the man she loved and would love all the rest of her life.

"You're the best thing that ever happened to me, Brittany," he said, becoming serious.

"How I love you!" she whispered. She leaned forward to kiss him—this tall, handsome man she would love forever.

* * * * *

Welcome to cowboy country...

Turn the page for a sneak preview of
TEXAS BABY
by Kathleen O'Brien
An exciting new title from Harlequin Superromance for
everyone who loves stories about the West.

Harlequin Superromance—
Where life and love weave together in emotional
and unforgettable ways.

CHAPTER ONE

CHASE TRANSFERRED his gaze to the road and identified a foreign spot on the horizon. A car. Almost half a mile away, where the straight, tree-lined drive met the public road. He could tell it was coming too fast, but judging the speed of a vehicle moving straight toward you was tricky.

It wasn't until it was about two hundred yards away that he realized the driver must be drunk...or crazy. Or both.

The guy was going maybe sixty. On a private drive, out here in ranch country, where kids or horses or tractors or stupid chickens might come darting out any minute, that was criminal. Chase straightened from his comfortable slouch and waved his hands.

"Slow down, you fool," he called out. He took the porch steps quickly and began walking fast down the driveway.

The car veered oddly, from one lane to another, then up onto the slight rise of the thick green spring grass. It just barely missed the fence.

"Slow down, damn it!"

He couldn't see the driver, and he didn't recognize this automobile. It was small and old, and couldn't have cost much, even when it was new. It was probably white, but now it needed either a wash or a new paint job, or both.

"Damn it, what's wrong with you?"

At the last minute, he had to jump away, because the idiot behind the wheel clearly wasn't going to turn to avoid a collision. He couldn't believe it. The car kept coming, finally slowing a little, but it was too late.

Still going about thirty miles an hour, it slammed into the large, white-brick pillar that marked the front boundaries of the house. The pillar wasn't going to give an inch, so the car had to. The front end folded up like a paper fan.

It seemed to take forever for the car to settle, as if the trauma happened in slow motion, reverberating from the front to the back of the car in ripples of destruction. The front windshield suddenly seemed to ice over with lethal bits of glassy frost. Then the side windows exploded.

The front driver's door wrenched open, as if the car wanted to expel its contents. Metal buckled hideously. Small pieces, like hubcaps and mirrors, skipped and ricocheted insanely across the oyster-shell driveway.

Finally, everything was still. Into the silence, a plume of steam shot up like a geyser, smelling of rust and heat. Its snake-like hiss almost smothered the low, agonized moan of the driver.

Chase's anger had disappeared. He didn't feel anything but a dull sense of disbelief. Things like this didn't happen in real life. Not in his life. Maybe the sun had actually put him to sleep....

But he was already kneeling beside the car. The driver was a woman. The frosty glass-ice of the windshield was dotted with small flecks of blood. She must have hit it with her head, because just below her hairline a red liquid was seeping out. He touched it. He tried to wipe it away before it reached her eyebrow, though, of course, that made no sense at all. Her eyes were shut.

Was she conscious? Did he dare move her? Her dress was covered in glass, and the metal of the car was sticking out lethally in all the wrong places.

Then he remembered, with an intense relief, that every good medical man in the county was here, just behind the house, drinking his champagne. He found his phone and paged Trent.

The woman moaned again.

Alive, then. Thank God for that.

He saw Trent coming toward him, starting out at a lope, but quickly switching to a full run.

"Get Dr. Marchant," Chase called. "Don't bother with 911."

Trent didn't take long to assess the situation. A fraction of a second, and he began pulling out his cell phone and running toward the house.

The yelling seemed to have roused the woman. She opened her eyes. They were blue and clouded with pain and confusion.

"Chase," she said.

His breath stalled. His head pulled back. "What?"

Her only answer was another moan, and he wondered if he had imagined the word. He reached around her and put his arm behind her shoulders. She was tiny. Probably petite by nature, but surely way too thin. He could feel her shoulder blades pushing against her skin, as fragile as the wishbone in a turkey.

She seemed to have passed out, so he put his other arm under her knees and lifted her out. He tried to avoid the jagged metal, but her skirt caught on a piece and the tearing sound seemed to wake her again.

"No," she said. "Please."

"I'm just trying to help," he said. "It's going to be all right."

She seemed profoundly distressed. She wriggled in his arms, and she was so weak, like a broken bird. It made him feel too big and brutish. And intrusive. As if touching her this way, his bare hands against the warm skin behind her knees, were somehow a transgression.

He wished he could be more delicate. But he smelled gasoline, and he knew it wasn't safe to leave her here.

Finally, he heard the sound of voices, as guests began to run around the side of the house, alerted by Trent. Dr. Marchant was at the front, racing toward them as if he were forty instead of seventy. Susannah was right behind him, her green dress floating around her trim legs.

"Please," the woman in his arms murmured again. She looked at him, the expression in her blue eyes lost and bewildered. He wondered if she might be on drugs. Hitting her head on the windshield might account for this unfocused, glazed look, but it couldn't explain the crazy driving.

"Please, put me down. Susannah… The wedding…"

Chase's arms tightened instinctively, and he froze in his tracks. She whimpered, and he realized he might be hurting her. "Say that again?"

"The wedding. I have to stop it."

* * * * *

Be sure to look for TEXAS BABY,
available September 11, 2007,
as well as other fantastic Superromance titles
available in September.

HARLEQUIN
Super Romance®

Welcome to Cowboy Country...

TEXAS BABY
by Kathleen O'Brien

#1441

Chase Clayton doesn't know what to think.
A beautiful stranger has just crashed his
engagement party, demanding that he not
marry because she's pregnant with his baby.
But the kicker is—he's never seen her before.

Look for TEXAS BABY and other fantastic
Superromance titles on sale September 2007.

Available wherever books are sold.

HARLEQUIN
Super Romance®

**Where life and love weave together
in emotional and unforgettable ways.**